THE BLACK ACCORDS EMERGENCE

DEAN MOSS

Book Design by HMD Publishing

To my dearest wife,
thank you for your love and patience.

CONTENTS

FIRST CONTACT

AMONG STRANGERS

POWER SHADOWS

PRESSURE FRONT

THE ACCORDS

PART I:

FIRST CONTACT

Chapter 1: JUDE BLACK

The morning light bled through the glass as if it weren't supposed to be there, as if even the sun needed permission to enter this part of Manhattan.

Jude stood at the edge of his corner office, thirty-seven floors above the Hudson's slow, uncertain shimmer. Behind him, the city breathed its usual rhythm: compressed, caffeinated, oblivious.

Beyond the river, the Statue of Liberty stood as it always had—immutable, pretending it still meant what it once did.

He didn't hate the view, but he didn't believe in it either.

He wore the kind of suit that made tailors feel seen: navy that looked charcoal in poor light, shoulders disciplined, cuffs clean. Sharp enough to be remembered, neutral enough to be forgotten. A fine white scar crossed the knuckle of his left hand, the only loud thing about him. It had never healed flat.

His face revealed no history—clean lines, a look that defaulted to unreadable. His hair was kept short, a quiet compromise.

When he moved, it was with the economy of someone who had learned early that excess was an admission.

Jude caught his reflection in the glass and, for a moment, the city doubled him, an echo layered over a man. He let the moment fade. Somewhere in his muscle memory, older than he liked, lingered the habit of refusing what tried to move him.

He sipped his coffee, black, and let the silence settle. These were the last few hours he would spend here, the final day before the move. A calculated relocation, nothing sentimental. London no longer felt like home; it was simply necessary.

A new role. More autonomy. A bigger footprint.

Officially, he would be heading up European strategy for the firm. Unofficially, he would be untethered—less watched, more dangerous. Which was the point.

He had it all mapped out. And he believed, in that moment, as the sun fought its way into his life one last time, that the plan would unfold exactly as he intended.

A knock sounded at the glass.

Jayden from the real estate investment team stood there, tie askew, blazer open, drink already in hand—bourbon, probably. He leaned against the doorway as if he owned the place, smiling like he had just caught Jude doing something deeply uncool.

"Come on, Black. We're not letting you ghost your own send-off. Whiskey's flowing, people are saying things they'll regret. You'll love it."

Jude didn't turn. "That sounds dreadful."

"Exactly. It's basically therapy, but with cheaper liquor."

Jude allowed the faintest of smirks; half-respect, half-weariness.

"They sent you to collect me?"

Jayden shrugged. "You were brooding at the glass wall like a Bond villain. Figured I'd better check before someone jumped."

"You good, man?" Jayden asked after a pause.

Jude finally looked at him. "I'm fine."

Jayden nodded, satisfied, though not quite convinced.

"Alright then. Grab your ego and let's go. I'm not finishing your bottle."

Jude glanced one last time at the Hudson, the river pretending to move. Then he turned away.

The next morning, Jude zipped the last of his luggage and let the click settle into the silence of the apartment.

It was early. Tribeca was still quiet, wrapped in the kind of light that made glass look like memory.

Behind him came soft footsteps.

A woman—brunette, barefoot, wearing one of his shirts—rubbed her eyes and gave him a lazy smile.

"Didn't think you'd be up before me."

"I don't sleep much," Jude said, still facing the window.

She stopped at the edge of the kitchen, fingers tracing the marble.

"You sure about London?"

"Never been unsure," he replied.

She nodded, stepped forward, and kissed him lightly on the cheek.

Friendly. Decidedly noncommittal.

"Last night was fun. But I'll still miss seeing you around."

Jude turned at that and smiled faintly.

"New York has enough ghosts. One less won't matter."

She laughed, quiet and genuine, before padding back toward the bedroom.

Jude lifted his bags, one in each hand, and paused at the door.

He didn't know then that this would be the last time his life felt ordinary. Beyond this moment, everything would shift. Somewhere on a quiet hillside, an ocean away, something older than myth was falling through the sky, straight into his path.

Chapter 2:
LONDON WELCOME

He hated Heathrow.

Not because of the noise, the lines, or the fluorescent lights that made everyone look like the inside of a plastic bag. He hated it because it always pretended to be more than it was—polished, modern, international—while beneath the surface it remained just a waiting room with better branding.

Still, it made for a clean entry point. Unremarkable. Which suited him.

Jude stepped through the arrivals gate with his carry-on slung over one shoulder, coat draped over the other. Crisp suit, collar open, not a wrinkle out of place.

He scanned the crowd and spotted her immediately.

His mother, Anne, waved with one hand while cradling her phone in the other. Even here, she was likely juggling emails for the foundation she chaired, one of those legacy trusts that always seemed to blur the lines between charity and influence. She looked like someone who belonged on a university brochure: elegant, unfazed by jet lag, perfectly pulled together.

Beside her stood his sister, Naomi. Arms folded, sharp blazer, hair in a precise bun that hadn't moved in years. She worked in PR, and even now seemed ready to step onto a panel or deliver a quote to the Times.

Jude approached with a smile that could be filed under polite professionalism.

"Well," Naomi said, eyeing him. "Still dressed like a finance bro. Good to know some things haven't changed."

"I missed your warmth," Jude replied dryly.

His mother leaned in and kissed him on the cheek.

"You look thin," she said. "Are you eating, or just intimidating baristas for breakfast?"

"It's a time-saver."

Naomi smirked.

"Dad's in Brussels," Anne added. "He said to tell you good luck and that he's glad you're at least orbiting home again. Whatever that means."

"Means he wants a photo op if I ever do anything vaguely patriotic," Jude said.

The drive from Heathrow to central London was calm, as if the city hadn't noticed he had left or returned. Jude sat in the back with his mother beside him, Naomi up front next to the driver, offering unsolicited critiques of everything from city traffic policy to Anne's upcoming charity auction.

"You should at least consider a launch dinner," Naomi said. "Put your name on the map in a softer way before the sharks sniff you out."

"I don't need soft," Jude replied, watching the buildings scroll past the window.

"No," Anne said. "But it wouldn't kill you to try appearing human."

"Strong branding starts with authenticity," Naomi chimed in.

Jude arched an eyebrow. "You're quoting yourself again."

"Only because no one else will."

They dropped him off just outside the firm's London office—a clean, glass-fronted building tucked discreetly into a Mayfair side street. New plaque. Quiet lobby. The kind of place designed to look modest from the outside and expensive within.

Anne stepped out, kissed his cheek again.

"Text when you're done. We'll have dinner on Tuesday."

"Assuming you're not halfway to Vienna by then," Jude replied.

Naomi leaned from the window.

"Try not to work so hard that they think you don't like people. You've got a whole new team to terrify."

"Noted."

Inside, the office was quiet but not still, the soft hum of expensive furniture, filtered air, and money moving discreetly. A glass partition framed the reception. Jude's name was already etched on the internal directory under Managing Partner, Europe.

A woman stood near the elevators, tablet in hand, posture straight, expression professionally unreadable.

"Mr. Black?" she said. "Welcome. I'm Faye, Chief of Staff here. The team's upstairs waiting to meet you."

"Lead the way."

The conference room was small but sleek, occupied by five people who rose the moment he entered.

He read them quickly.

Alex, the operations lead, mid-thirties. Probably an ex-banker; alert, calculating.

Claire, junior partner. Impeccably dressed, sharp eyes, already planning the next five meetings.

Mihir, tech-side lead. Lean, quiet, hoodie that all but announced Oxford dropout.

Danika, investor relations. Poised, with a smile you couldn't trust but couldn't ignore.

Hugo, the old hand. Grey at the temples, smile more reserved than warm.

"Morning," Jude said, setting his bag down. "You've probably heard too much about me already. Hopefully most of it's true."

A few chuckles, polite nods.

"We were just saying," Claire began, "how nice it is to have someone who understands both New York scale and London tact."

"Translation," Hugo added, "we assume you don't sleep."

"Sleep's inefficient," Jude said. "I prefer clarity."

That drew more laughter. Ice cracked, but didn't quite melt.

"We've got a short team lunch scheduled," Faye offered. "Nothing formal, just a chance to connect."

Jude nodded, checking his watch.

"Sounds good. Let's keep it short. Plenty to do."

They filed out together, a procession of poised sharks circling a new current.

Jude lingered by the conference room window. Outside, London stretched like a machine that didn't know it had been restarted.

He liked the view. But he didn't believe in it either.

He didn't know, of course, that this would be the last week the world would run on autopilot. That far beyond London, something that didn't belong here was about to arrive, and it wouldn't knock first.

Chapter 3:
OLD FRIENDS

The flat belonged to Tom's uncle, though Tom had somehow managed to live there for two years without paying rent or learning how to use the dishwasher.

It was the kind of place you didn't really furnish, just inherited tastefully. Wide-planked oak floors, high ceilings, and bookshelves untouched since the last Labour government. Bottles of whisky sat on a glass tray like museum pieces. A record player hummed faintly in the corner, spinning something vintage and French.

Jude arrived just before nine. He lingered outside for a moment, standing in the glow of the entryway light. Across the street, a couple laughed softly, arms linked. They slipped into a taxi without noticing him.

The intercom buzzed before he pressed it.

Adeel's voice came through, exaggerated and bright.

"If that's not Jude Black, tell him to piss off unless he brought better wine."

Jude smirked and let himself in.

Inside, the flat was already half a party, coats on chairs, glasses everywhere, laughter bouncing off brick and wood. The kind of chaos old friendships carried on muscle memory.

"Look what the private jet dragged in," Mike called from the kitchen, swirling a glass of red that looked too expensive for him to have bought himself.

Tom, barefoot and loose-limbed, waved lazily from the couch where he sat cross-legged in gym clothes that had never seen a gym.

"Your flat too minimalist for human contact, Black?"

"It's only minimalist when I know what I'm missing," Jude replied, stepping inside and shrugging out of his coat.

Leo appeared beside him, offering a drink Jude didn't remember asking for.

"Missed you, mate," Leo said, pulling him in briefly. "Still scheming for world domination?"

Jude took the drink. "Still lying like a politician."

There were hugs, handshakes, shoulder squeezes—the same dance they had all done a dozen times before.

And then, Ella.

She stood near the window with Nate, half-listening as he explained something about orbital debris and how everyone misunderstands low-earth satellites. She wore a dark green jumper, sleeves pushed to her elbows, glass in hand. Casual. Effortless.

She turned as Jude approached.

"Hey, stranger," she said.

"Hey," Jude replied, careful not to look too long.

"London treating you like a local yet?"

"I've already been offered bad coffee and unsolicited political opinions. So yes."

She smiled, one corner only, familiar but reserved.

"Still sharp."

"Still German."

"Touché."

They were interrupted by Rosie, crashing between them with a glass in one hand and a half-eaten breadstick in the other.

"Can we play the question game, please? I'm bored of men talking about space and money."

"That's because you don't understand either," Nate replied with a grin.

"I understand plenty," Rosie said, turning to Jude. "For example, who here do you think peaked in secondary school?"

Tom raised his hand.

"I peaked in Year Ten. Been downhill since I got that prefect badge."

"What about Jude?" Mike said. "He's peaking now, surely. You're the guy everyone thinks is dating a Rothschild and secretly buying the moon."

"No comment," Jude said.

Adeel appeared with a speaker.

"Enough talk. Music time. Jude, you still like tragic synth, or have you evolved?"

"Only if the lyrics make me question my life choices."

"Perfect," Adeel said. "I have just the playlist."

The night blurred into laughter, old school stories, half-serious accusations of cheating on exams, and one tale about Leo nearly being expelled for sneaking into the girls' dorm, a story no one could ever confirm.

Mike filled doorways without trying, broad-shouldered, with the gentle, lopsided smile he used when he knew he'd overstepped and planned to do it again. Shirt untucked, watch scuffed. He hugged like a full stop.

Tom was all angles and momentum: wiry, barefoot, boyish, with a laugh that arrived before the joke. He gestured when he spoke, drawing maps in the air only he could read.

Nate looked like he had once remembered sleep and let it go. Lean, glasses slipping, cardigan doing its best. Fingers faintly stained from a pen he never admitted was leaking. Speech precise until it wandered into space and refused to return.

Leo carried a consultant's polish trim beard, perfect collar, and shoes that never touched rain if he could help it. A quickness in his eyes weighed a room like a spreadsheet.

Adeel wore charm like a tailored coat: effortless, amused, dangerous in court. He collected stories the way others collected debts, and paid in punchlines.

They were a pattern you could recognize blindfolded. Familiar enough that no one noticed the edges they carried.

Later, as the night thinned and the group sprawled lazily with their drinks, Jude found himself on the balcony with Ella again.

The air was cooler now, the street quieter. A bus hummed in the distance.

"Still don't like crowds?" she asked.

"They're tolerable when they know how to pour wine."

"You were different back then, you know. Louder. Less... managed."

Jude took a breath, watching a plane blink across the sky.

"Maybe I just learned when to be quiet."

"That's not the same as learning to listen."

Ella tucked a stray strand of brunette hair behind her ear, the motion unbothered, automatic. In this light, the green of her eyes seemed to steal color from the city and keep it. Her mouth did half-smiles better than full ones; economy of expression as policy.

Up close, her English carried the shape of another language, a crispness on consonants, a refusal to waste a word. She wore practical rings, nothing that asked to be announced.

He remembered the message she had once sent at two in the morning: a photo of a desk buried in articles, captioned I miss the part where data behaves. She had left a doctoral program that didn't deserve her patience and never filed the last paper. The department called it a deferral. She called it learning to walk away from systems that mistake control for care.

He admired that. Walking away had never come easily to him. Maybe that was why he kept looking at her longer than he meant to.

"Listening is a skill," she said, eyes on the street.

"And a choice," he said.

"That too," she allowed, and the corner of her mouth conceded the point.

They stood in silence for a moment.

"Still coming on the hike?" he asked. "Claire from my office is coming too. Apparently, she and Tom know each other well."

"Still deciding whether I want to see any of you in thermals."

"That's fair."

"But yeah," she added, softer. "Wouldn't miss it."

Later, back inside, the group was collapsing into jackets and leftover crisps. Nate tried to organize a shared car. Mike refused to ride in anything Leo was driving. Rosie threatened to hike barefoot just to prove a point.

Tom, sprawled across the couch again, yawned dramatically.

"Right. Countryside it is. If we all die in a forest together, at least it'll be aesthetic."

Jude smiled, but felt it in his spine.

He wasn't sure why, but something was shifting; something old, quiet, and coming fast.

That night, before bed, he checked his phone.

[**Ella**]: *Just done packing. You better not bail.*

[**Jude**]: *If I disappear, you're in charge of blaming Tom.*

[**Ella**]: *Deal.*

Chapter 4:
AUTUMN TRIP

Packing was chaos.

Tom insisted he knew where the hiking permits were. He didn't. Mike forgot a sleeping bag, borrowed one from Rosie, and immediately complained about the color. Adeel brought a Bluetooth speaker, two bottles of champagne, and no socks.

Jude, naturally, was packed by seven.

He stepped out of his Chelsea flat an hour later, just as Tom's Range Rover pulled up crookedly at the curb, music pulsing faintly from inside. It was already a mess: bags everywhere, a cool box wedged where someone's legs should have been, Rosie's scarf tied around the mirror for no reason at all.

"Get in, mate," Mike called from the back. "We're going hiking!"

Jude loaded his gear into the boot with silent efficiency and claimed the front passenger seat. Ella was already there, sipping coffee from a thermos, hair tied back, hoodie zipped halfway.

"You're late," she said, without looking at him.

"I was early. You were all late."

She glanced over with a faint smile. "So punctual it's antisocial."

Tom pulled away with far too much confidence and far too little regard for the handbrake.

The road out of London was grey and functional. Suburbs gave way to motorways, fields, and the kind of English countryside that looked like it had stopped trying to impress.

The SUV rumbled on, filled with too much noise for Jude's liking—podcast debates, clumsy playlist transitions, and Rosie loudly explaining why she no longer trusted clouds.

Somewhere past Guildford, Nate launched into an earnest breakdown of a recent aerospace bid.

"It's not just the funding model," he said. "It's about launch cadence. Everyone's too obsessed with rockets and not enough with payload interface. Give it ten years and ground stations will matter more than..."

"Nate," Adeel interrupted from the middle row, "if you say one more word about orbital infrastructure, I'm launching you into a field."

"Try me," Nate said, smiling. "You wouldn't last a week without Starlink."

"If that's a threat," Mike muttered, "I hope the aliens take you first."

Laughter. Music. Then, eventually, stillness.

By noon, they pulled into a fuel station outside a village with three buildings and a single pub named The Dead Drake.

While Tom fueled up, Jude drifted toward a ridge behind the lot. It was quiet, too quiet for his comfort. The air felt thinner. Lighter. Almost waiting.

He paused. Listened.

Somewhere in the distance came a faint metallic hum, not loud, but distinct. It vanished as quickly as it arrived.

"You alright?" Ella asked behind him.

He turned. She held out a protein bar.

"You looked like you were seeing ghosts."

"I don't believe in ghosts," he said.

"That's the problem."

She handed him the bar and walked back toward the car.

Jude stayed for a few more seconds, frowning at the sky. The clouds weren't moving right. They dragged sideways, as if the air had changed its rules.

The last stretch of the drive wound them past Old Winchester Hill, open country layered in pale green and brown. Long dry-stone walls divided the fields like scars from an older time.

By the time they pulled into the gravel drive near the Georgian manor, the sun was trying and failing to break through.

Their chosen stay, the estate's secluded renovated barn, was modern rustic: glass and timber, minimalist with countryside guilt. Jude carried his own gear while the others argued over rooms. Adeel claimed the one with the freestanding bath; Rosie traded him for the one with the skylight.

Jude didn't care. He chose the corner room and unpacked with clinical ease.

Later, as they prepped dinner—or rather, watched Ella and Rosie do everything while pretending to help—the laughter returned.

There was wine, cheap music, and a group selfie where only three people looked good. Normalcy. Rhythm.

Then came the moment.

Just after nine, Jude stepped outside for air.

The sky had turned to grey milk, heavy with something unspoken. He looked up just in time to catch it: a faint, silent streak burning across the sky, not falling, not arcing, but clean, deliberate, controlled.

He stared.

No sound. No trail. Just a shimmer that vanished behind the tree line.

"Did you see that?" he called.

Mike and Tom were dragging firewood over.

"What, that shooting star thing?"

"It wasn't..." Jude stopped. "Yeah. Sure."

"Make a wish," Tom said. "I wish this fire actually lights."

The others didn't seem to care. Why would they? To them, it was only light in the sky.

Jude said nothing more.

But he felt it. A weight. A shift. The sense that the world had been nudged, not broken, just rebalanced.

He looked toward the hills beyond the field.

Something had come through.

Chapter 5:
HAMPSHIRE INCIDENT

The morning air bit harder than expected.

They set out just after eight, boots crunching over frost-glazed grass, breath fogging the space between jokes and complaints. The sky was pale and expressionless, as if it had been wiped clean overnight.

Ella, Rosie, and Claire had opted to stay behind—tea, books, and, as they put it, "not wanting to pretend this was a military exercise." No one argued.

The trail climbed slowly, cutting through woodland just wet enough to be slippery. Birds called in odd, uneven bursts. The silence between them stretched too long.

"It's weirdly quiet," Mike muttered.

"That's nature for you," Leo replied. "Passive-aggressive."

"This is how people vanish in documentaries," Adeel added.

The laughter came light, but Jude wasn't listening. Not fully.

An hour in, they stopped at a ridge for water and breath. That's when Jude saw it.

Down the next slope lay a fresh gash in the earth, maybe twenty meters long, as if the hill had been peeled open by something not entirely physical.

"You see that?" he asked, pointing.

The others followed his gaze.

“Storm erosion?” Tom offered, squinting.

“Too clean,” Nate said, already moving downhill. “Let’s check it out.”

They moved slowly, steps more cautious now.

At the base of the incline they found the impact site: a shallow trench, dark soil peeled back like black velvet. At the far end, half-buried in mud, lay a smooth, matte black object—angular, alien, wrong.

Not mechanical. Not natural. Just there.

“That is not from here,” Mike said.

“Military test drone?” Leo offered weakly.

“Not with that geometry,” Nate muttered. “That surface texture…”

No one stepped closer.

Jude did.

Something in him shifted—not drawn, not called, but pressed. He crouched at the edge of the object.

It pulsed once, softly.

And the world vanished.

The expanse

White. Total. Soundless.

Jude stood barefoot in the impossible light, breathing hard. His chest felt hollow. Time, if it existed, crawled in every direction at once.

He wasn’t alone.

A figure emerged from the void, shifting, humanoid, indistinct. No features. No weight. Only intent.

Designated host acquired.

The voice wasn't heard. It was experienced.

Commencing containment.

A cage began to rise around him. Thin white columns spiraled upward in synchronized order, forming a shell that tightened with each breath.

He couldn't move. Panic flickered. His muscles refused him.

Then—

He pushed.

Not a conscious act, but something deeper, older. A refusal. A crack in submission.

The cage stuttered. A plate misaligned. The light dimmed.

Unexpected resistance.

Jude clenched his fists. The cage wavered. Bent.

The figure stepped forward, too fast, and slammed into him.

They fell.

Not standing now, but wrestling in weightless silence. No sound, only flashes of white, pressure, speed. Hands gripped. Shoulders collided. Jude's mind screamed voicelessly as the figure tried to re-assert control.

You are not in control.

Jude twisted, drove a shoulder, shoved the figure back, breaking free for half a breath.

And something changed.

New lines rose. Not around him, but around *it.*

A new cage, different in shape. Faster. Stronger. Aggressive.

White blades of thought and form closed around the figure, trapping it.

The being lunged again, hit the bars, and reeled back. Static sparked across its now-skeletal frame.

No. No. No.

The bars slammed shut.

Jude gasped.

The forest rushed back—color, sound, weight.

He was on his knees in the cold mud, chest heaving, hands shaking.

Around him, the others stirred.

Nate stood first. Then Adeel. Then Leo, Mike and Tom. One by one, in quiet succession, like marionettes remembering they had strings.

Their eyes were wrong.

Not glazed. Not blank.

Focused. Composed. Inhabited.

Jude pushed himself upright slowly, every joint aching. Something pressed behind his eyes, not pain, but presence.

Then a voice, not his own, rose inside him.

Not words exactly. More like a thought forced into his mind from behind a wall.

"Remain still. Do not speak unless required. They believe you are one of us.

Jude's heart pounded.

"They do not yet know you resisted. That I… failed to complete integration. If they realize it, they will eliminate you. And me with you."

The others were upright now, dusting themselves off, checking their limbs.

Then Nate spoke.

"This body is viable. Musculature intact. No internal rupture."

Leo stepped forward, stretching his arms with mechanical precision.

"Language calibration at eighty percent. Locomotion stable. No neural degradation."

Adeel examined his hands, then lifted his gaze toward the horizon.

"Atmospheric intake compatible. Sight range acceptable. Local temperature... inefficient."

Jude stayed silent.

Inside, the voice pressed again, tighter now, measured.

"You must not draw suspicion. Mimic their cadence. Let them believe you were taken fully. If they kill this vessel, I am lost. And so are you."

The five others turned toward him.

Mike tilted his head slightly.

"You recovered more slowly."

Jude stood, steadying himself. His voice came quiet, calculated.

"Cognitive integration required adjustment."

They accepted that. No nods. Just a shared pause, then movement.

Together, they began walking back toward the trail.

Not as friends.

Not as people.

But as something else.

Jude followed, the only human mind among a group no longer fully human.

And deep inside him, the thing that had tried to consume him now sat contained. Silent for now. Watching.

As he walked, Jude closed his eyes. The cold vanished. The silence returned.

And he stood once more in the white expanse.

The cage glowed faintly before him.

The figure inside was watching.

Jude met its gaze.

"Who are you?"

PART II:

AMONG STRANGERS

Chapter 6:
TAKRA VAEL

The chamber was warm. Artificially so, the environment was engineered to match the final threshold of the ancient Aethero homeworld's atmosphere, or so the myth claimed. Comfort, in a sterile form.

Vael stood beneath the transfer cradle, arms loose at his sides, breath steady. His ceremonial mantle had been folded and placed aside. No symbols would accompany him. No armor. No identity but thought.

Above him, the vessel waited, smooth and inert, its black frame suspended in containment fields like a blade poised to be thrown.

Seven would descend from his clan.

Only seven.

Kareth approached, uniform and precise, expression taut with reverence.

"Takra, suul atrin vellan." *Grand Marshal, the final sequence is aligned.*

"I am ready."

Kareth bowed slightly. The pause that followed was not protocol; it was personal.

"The cause is sacred. The risk is... acknowledged."

"Vekan thuaral." *We ascend by fire.*

Kareth withdrew, leaving to prepare himself for the journey as well.

Then the doors opened again.

Lyren entered without clearance, but with purpose. She walked like someone with nothing to lose.

"They'll write hymns about you," she said. "But not all of them will be songs of praise."

"Then let them sing in dissonance," Vael replied.

She stepped closer, her voice low.

"This is exile, Vael. The moment you leave this body, the High Circle will move without you."

"It must. That is the point."

"Not all agree with the Circle anymore," she said. "They look to someone who acts, not just one who hides behind propaganda."

"You're speaking of dissent."

"I'm speaking of transition."

She held his gaze.

"Tharan isek..." *You could lead them...*

"Not yet," Vael said. "Let them see what I see. Then let them decide."

She didn't argue. She turned and left.

Kareth returned.

"Last designation? Linguistic alignment?"

Vael looked up, resolute.

"No compression. I speak as myself."

Kareth inclined his head.

"We go beyond the threshold, Vael."

The cradle sealed with a hiss of containment vapor. Lights dimmed to pale blue. Cold surged across his spine like water through the soul.

Core-thread anchor disengaging... Consciousness isolating...

Memory sequence in motion... Essence transferring...

No breath. No heartbeat.

No self.

Only momentum.

The expanse

When awareness returned, it was light.

White.

Endless.

He hovered in a space between self and silence, between purpose and thought.

And then the tether came.

A mind, primitive, unfiltered, but powerful.

He began integration.

Containment formed. The host would bend.

"It must bend."

But the host pushed back.

Hard.

The cage stuttered, then collapsed.

He was thrown.

Pain wasn't the right word, but something close to dissonance rippled through him.

He tried again. Lunged for control.

But the mind struck back, not with precision, but with raw will.

A cage rose, not around the human, but around Vael.

"This is not the protocol. This is not the plan."

White bars locked in.

He reeled, pinned in light.

Now he watches. Trapped. Present, but powerless.

The others stir. Their vessels hold.

He whispers to the human, low and urgent:

"Do not reveal yourself. Let them believe I succeeded. If they destroy this body, I perish with it."

Movement returns.

The host—Jude, he would later learn—begins walking again.

And then:

"Who are you?"

The voice is quiet. Calm. Unyielding.

Vael looked back through the bars.

And for the first time in many cycles, he didn't know the answer.

Chapter 7: VESSELS

They stood just outside the barn, the hills fading under a bruised sky.

The air had turned sharp, carrying the scent of churned soil and dry pine needles. No one spoke.

Then Jude did.

He turned to the five others, his friends, now strangers, and said in a voice he barely recognized as his own:

"Vel'at sha-threk. Em'koran tam alun." *Maintain human function. We act normal for now.*

The air felt rearranged. Not louder. Not brighter. Just other, as though someone had redrawn the outlines and left him to walk through them.

He became aware of details he had never asked for: the rough weave of his shirt against the skin at his collar, the uneven rhythm of his own breathing, the way silence seemed to carry a pattern beneath it.

It wasn't power. It was perspective, like standing beside someone who pointed out constellations you had never noticed. Once shown, they were impossible to unsee.

Jude blinked once. Nothing around him had changed. And yet, nothing would ever be ordinary again.

Inside his head, the voice whispered, not cruelly, not kindly:

"Repeat after me. Say it clearly. Let them hear the rhythm."

He felt it again, the strange mental echo of Vael guiding his tongue.

Leo nodded first.

Nate repeated the words softly.

Tom, Adeel, and Mike followed without hesitation.

Jude turned and led them toward the barn. His limbs felt heavier with each step. Every door, every patch of floor, every object inside carried new weight, like it belonged to a reality already slipping away.

The barn felt colder than it had that morning.

Jude crossed the threshold behind the others, boots caked in mud, the scent of pine and damp grass still clinging to his coat. The sun was already sliding low behind the hills, casting golden stripes through the wide glass panes along the west wall.

Inside, the others dispersed with unnatural efficiency.

Nate went directly to the kitchen.

Leo and Tom sat side by side on the edge of the sofa, silent.

Mike pulled a tablet from his bag, scrolling as if searching for data no one had given him.

No complaints about sore feet.

No jokes.

No "someone make tea" or "whose turn is it to cook."

"Too smooth," Jude thought. *"Too coordinated."*

He caught Adeel's glance. The nod that followed wasn't a greeting but an acknowledgment. Jude mirrored it, one nod, no words, no signal.

And that was the game now.

"Do not break form," the voice whispered, calm and cold inside his mind. *"They believe I succeeded. You are expected to perform as planned. Do not make me protect you from your own body."*

Jude didn't answer.

He took the same seat he had the night before, a corner armchair facing the fireplace. It felt wrong now. Smaller. Sharper.

From the hallway, a door creaked.

Ella stepped in first, followed by Rosie and Claire. Ella held a chipped mug, her thick jumper mismatched with her usual polish, hair tied back. She froze for half a second when she saw them, then kept walking, her rhythm easy again.

"Well," she said, raising an eyebrow. "Looks like nobody died. Good job."

No one replied.

"Okay," Rosie muttered. "What happened out there?"

Mike looked up. "The hike was... effective."

Claire tilted her head. "Effective at what? Cardio? Mutual silence therapy?"

Still no answer.

Ella frowned. "Is that supposed to be some kind of group improv bit? Because it's not funny."

Jude smiled, measured, calm.

"Everyone's knackered. Something about the forest, too quiet. Got us a bit introspective."

Ella squinted. "You alright?"

"Fine," Jude said. "Tired, that's all."

"You look pale."

"Cold air," he said.

"Hmm."

She walked to the stove and poured water into a kettle.

"Didn't hear much from the woods. One fox, I think. Maybe a deer."

Tom nodded stiffly. "There was wildlife."

Leo added, "Minimal disturbance. Environmental stability remains."

Rosie frowned. "Did you all bump your heads out there?"

The silence hung heavy.

Jude forced a short chuckle. "Too much oxygen. You'd be amazed how introspective five men get surrounded by trees."

Ella narrowed her eyes. But she smiled, half-convinced, half-curious.

"She is observant," the voice warned. *"You must distance her. Disrupt her trust."*

"No," Jude thought. *"I need her trust."*

The kettle boiled. With tea poured and shared around, the women disappeared into Rosie's room with quiet frowns. Jude remained in the corner chair. The others barely moved.

Nate's pen scratched steadily across paper.

Mike hadn't blinked in minutes.

Tom and Leo stared at the fireplace as if waiting for it to ignite itself.

Jude rose.

He moved through the barn with measured steps, making just enough noise to seem normal. No one followed. No one asked where he was going.

He stepped into the back hallway and closed the door to the utility room behind him.

Silence.

He shut his eyes.

The expanse's white void waited for him, unchanged as if it had never left.

The cage stood as before, thin bars of thought and geometry, pulsing with the quiet energy of containment.

Inside, the figure was clearer now. Humanoid in outline, smooth, featureless. Still watching.

Jude stepped forward, hesitant.

"*Who are you?*" he had asked earlier.

Only now the voice answered, not with noise, but through layers of thought:

"We are Aethero. We are the path that did not yield. The ones who chose self-determination over slavery. I was Takra Vael of the First Regiment. Now I am... here."

"You were supposed to take me over."

"You were supposed to yield."

"Why Earth?"

A pause.

"Your world lies within a forbidden sphere: protected, unsalvaged. But it is viable. Its climate aligns with our form. Its biology offers compatibility. Its defenses are primitive. It was deemed... inefficient to wait."

"So you broke your own rules."

"Not mine."

"You led the incursion?"

"I was sent to command it."

Jude stared at the cage. *"And now?"*

"Now we are both compromised. You contain me. I advise you. If they suspect, they will destroy you. And me with you."

"Despite you being their commander."

"Their Takra."

"You let me speak... Aethero," Jude said. *"You helped me survive."*

"I preserved myself," the voice replied. *"If you die, I vanish."*

"But you still haven't told me the plan."

A pause. Calculated.

"There are others. Other vessels. Other minds seeded across this world. Not all were meant to land in one place."

Jude's expression didn't shift.

"How many?"

"More than one."

"Who leads them?"

"Before impact, I did."

Jude stepped closer to the cage.

"And now?"

"Now I'm in a cage, speaking to the one mind that shouldn't have resisted. Now they will question. And some will challenge. And if they win, this planet burns."

"You need me."

"And you need me."

They stood in silence.

"Tell me more," Jude said.

"Later."

"No," Jude replied coolly. *"Now."*

"If you listen, I can help you survive. If you deceive them, you may even take control."

Jude said nothing. He only watched the figure shift within the bars, its form reshaping slightly, adapting again.

"We were never meant to speak like this," Vael said. *"But perhaps this is what your kind calls... a negotiation."*

The cage dimmed, retreating. Vael's shape blurred, less distinct. The connection faded.

Jude opened his eyes.

The hallway light had shifted, dusk falling fast.

A sound behind him.

He turned.

Ella.

She stood in the doorway, leaning against the frame, arms crossed.

"Everything okay?"

Jude nodded once. "Just needed quiet."

"So you chose the utility room?"

"No one thinks to look here."

She smiled faintly, but her eyes were sharp.

"You're not acting like yourself."

He didn't respond.

"Neither are the others. They're... coordinated. Like they're all waiting for something."

Jude met her gaze. "What do you think they're waiting for?"

"You," she said.

"I think they're waiting for you to decide."

Later that evening, they gathered in the main room again.

The fire crackled, though no one remembered who lit it. The overhead lights buzzed faintly. Jude sat where he had earlier, in the corner armchair, still watching.

Ella stood by the window with Claire, pretending to scroll through her phone, though the screen hadn't changed in ten minutes.

Nate kept sketching. Mike and Leo sat shoulder to shoulder, occasionally glancing toward the kitchen door, though nothing ever came through it. Adeel muttered lines of dialogue under his breath, rehearsed, as if testing words.

Tom finally spoke.

"Tomorrow we explore the upper ridgeline."

"Forecast says rain," Jude replied casually.

Tom blinked. "Adaptable."

"You okay with that?" Jude asked, turning toward Adeel.

Adeel's head tilted. "Rain is water. Water is non-lethal in most forms."

Ella shot Jude a look.

He stood. "Ella, want to help me check the food situation?"

"Sure," she said quickly, maybe too quickly.

They stepped into the kitchen. Jude closed the door behind them.

Ella leaned against the counter. "Okay, I know I joke about cult vibes sometimes, but this is genuinely creeping me out."

Jude opened a cupboard. "What's your read?"

"They're all... too aware. No filler talk. No idle fidgeting. They're saying things that don't match their personalities." She lowered her voice. "And it's not just weird. It's off. Like they've been rehearsing how to be people but keep forgetting the details."

Jude didn't answer. He pulled out a tin of chickpeas and handed it to her.

"Do something with this?"

She raised an eyebrow. "Are you testing my survival instincts?"

"More like kitchen diplomacy."

She turned toward the stove. "Do you trust them?"

He said nothing.

Instead, he stepped back into the main room alone and walked straight to Nate.

He was drawing. Lines. Not random. Geometric. Complex.

Jude leaned back slowly, angling for a better view.

A cube. Then an octagon. Then... a symbol. Not letters. Not human.

He blinked.

Vael didn't speak with Jude, but he watched.

"What are you drawing?"

Nate didn't look up. "Trajectory matrices. Object design extrapolation. Collision angle interpretation."

"For what?"

"The descent pattern. The vessels. The others."

"Others?"

Nate paused.

Then he looked up, eyes unblinking. "The five vessels."

Jude held his stare.

Nate blinked once. "I require food."

He stood, too smoothly, and walked toward the kitchen.

Jude remained crouched, staring at the notebook.

The symbols had shifted.

One looked disturbingly close to the Aethero glyphs he'd seen in the white expanse, the one Vael had called *kor'nai*. Soul-state. Essence in transition.

He looked up again. The room felt like it was tilting. The game was still on, but the board was much larger than he had realized. And he wasn't the only one playing.

He got up and went to check on Tom, and found him sitting cross-legged in the upstairs hallway, eyes wide and fixed on the wood grain beneath him.

"Hey," Jude said.

Tom didn't look up.

"I was trying to remember what pain feels like," he said flatly.

Jude stayed silent.

"The host had a memory," Tom continued. "Football. Dislocated shoulder. Screamed into his own mouth, he said."

"Sounds unpleasant."

Tom tilted his head.

"Would you scream?"

"I don't plan on needing to."

A long pause followed.

Then, still not looking at him, Tom said:

"I think the others will. Before the end."

Jude stared at him.

A thousand possibilities raced through his mind. He chose none of them.

"Sleep," Jude said coldly.

Tom didn't move. But Jude turned and walked away, quietly filing the words as both threat and warning.

Back downstairs, Jude stood at the head of the kitchen island with a decision made based on his observations of Nate and Tom.

The others were scattered loosely around the lounge, but only the girls were talking.

Rosie was mid-rant about Leo's silence at dinner. Claire scrolled through weather reports. Ella leaned against the wall, arms folded, watching Jude.

He raised a hand slightly to get their attention.

"Change of plans. We're heading back to London tomorrow."

Claire frowned. "What? Why?"

"Some of us have last-minute work commitments. And the weather's about to turn ugly anyway."

"Wasn't this whole weekend meant to be the big switch-off?" Rosie asked.

"It still is," Jude said. "Just... in a different setting."

The boys stayed quiet.

Ella said, "Right. Because Leo's allergic to cloud cover."

No one laughed.

Jude gave a single nod. "Pack in the morning. We'll head out before noon."

He walked away before more questions could follow and stepped out onto the rear deck.

The air was cold and still, lit only by the last silver wash of twilight. The night pressed down with that strange quiet of rural places, where silence became its own sound.

Behind him, the door clicked softly.

Ella stepped out, arms folded, eyes narrowed.

"Don't lie to me."

Jude turned, calm, steady.

"I haven't said anything to lie about."

"Exactly," she snapped. "You always talk. Especially when something's off, and now it's like you're... mimicking yourself. Slightly off-script. Like they are."

He held her gaze, unreadable.

"You're paranoid," he said. "That's not always a weakness."

"And you're performing," she shot back. "But I don't think it's for me."

A pause.

"I'm managing a situation."

"That's not cryptic at all."

He finally tilted his head, meeting her eyes.

"If I told you something impossible happened, would you believe me?"

"Try me."

Jude studied her face.

"Not yet," he said.

"Then why are you telling me anything at all?"

"Because if something goes wrong, I need someone who remembers who I was."

She blinked. Whatever she had expected, it wasn't that.

Then: "You've scared me. Officially."

Jude didn't apologize. He just gave a single nod.

"What happened out there?"

"We saw something."

"What kind of something?"

"The kind you don't describe unless you're sure the person asking is ready to hear it."

She looked like she wanted to say more, but didn't.

"Pack early. We leave before noon."

She shook her head and stepped back inside. Jude waited a full minute before following.

That night, he lay on the mattress in the corner room, still fully dressed, eyes open. The voice came again.

"You are becoming entangled."

"I'm managing risk."

"You risk distraction. She will compromise you."

"Or she'll give me an edge when your people start to move against me."

A pause.

"You believe you are in control. You are not."

"I've held you in a cage since impact."

"Only because I allowed the moment to pass."

Jude smirked and shot back: *"Keep telling yourself that."*

A flicker of tension pulsed inside his skull. Not pain, just pressure.

Then silence.

The morning mist hung heavy.

Jude woke early. He hadn't truly slept.

He moved quietly through the barn, stepping over the last cold embers of the fire, past Leo and Mike, both still awake, still sitting where they had been the night before.

He opened the side door near the kitchen and stepped out into the chill.

That's when he saw Nate.

He was standing at the base of the property's old uplink mast, a relic from the barn's past life as a weather station.

Nate held his phone, its screen glowing faint green, angled toward a metal junction box.

Jude walked up behind him, calm.

"What are you doing?"

Nate didn't flinch.

"Transmitting environmental data. Seismic readings. Biosphere equilibrium."

"To whom?"

Nate turned slowly. "Unknown."

Jude took the phone from his hand.

The screen was dark. No app open. Battery at 78 percent. No network icon.

"Go inside," Jude said.

Nate hesitated.

"Now."

He obeyed, silently.

Jude stood alone in the fog, holding the cold, blank phone.

"That was not my instruction," Vael said in his mind. *"That signal was improvised. Unscheduled."*

"Then who gave him permission?"

"Kareth," Vael answered.

For the first time, the name dropped like a weight between them.

"He's inside Mike, isn't he?"

"Correct. He was second among the descent core. Loyal. Capable."

"Still loyal?"

"For now. But his interpretation of the mission may diverge if your behavior proves... inconsistent."

"So I act like you."

"Precisely."

"And if I don't?"

"He'll see it as contamination."

"How many vessels made it?"

A pause.

"Five were sent. Scattered. Each with a primary function and local discretion, in key states that form what you call the United Nations Security Council. I was the central node. The planner. The others were given autonomy, should I be lost. You stopped me. Now they will believe leadership is... undecided."

"And if they find out I'm not you?"

"Then they will eliminate you. And Earth."

Jude stared at the relay.

"You want your command intact. I want my friends to live."

"Then we are aligned. Temporarily."

"Then we play it my way."

The mist hadn't lifted. Pale light cut through the trees, but the air still held the damp, grey weight of the night before.

Jude loaded his bag into the van first. The others followed in practiced rhythm.

Mike—Kareth—was last. He gave Jude a quiet nod.

"Trajectories adjusted. Urban deployment will resume upon arrival."

"Don't deviate," Jude said flatly.

"Deviation implies disorder. I intend neither."

The response was flawless. But Jude caught the flicker in his eyes. The calculation.

"He's watching you now," Vael said.

"Let him," Jude replied. *"He'll misread the results."*

Claire and Rosie were already seated, chatting lightly, unaware, or pretending to be.

Ella stood beside the van, one hand wrapped around her thermos, eyes locked on Jude.

"London, huh?" she said.

"It's safer to be in familiar places," Jude replied.

"You don't believe that."

"No. But they do."

She held his gaze for a second longer, then climbed inside.

Jude lingered by the door.

"You're learning," Vael said. *"You speak as though you believe your own lies."*

"That's how they become real."

He shut the door and started the engine.

Hours later, London's skyline rose like steel teeth through the haze. The Shard pierced low cloud. Red buses slid through traffic. Everything looked exactly as it should, and nothing felt real.

Nate was in the front passenger seat, showing an unnatural interest in the GPS system. The girls talked quietly in the back row.

Jude kept his eyes on Mike through the rearview mirror. Kareth wore the body well. He blinked when needed. Smiled when spoken to. His posture was flawless.

Too flawless.

"His rhythms are slightly accelerated," Vael said. *"He's calibrating for urban density. Watching patterns."*

"So am I," Jude replied.

They dropped off the girls first. Ella lingered.

"You going to tell me what really happened?"

"Not today."

"Will there be a day?"

"If there's time."

She frowned. "You always talk like you know the ending."

Jude gave the faintest smile. "I'm just rarely surprised."

She left with no further word.

When Jude finally got to his quiet flat, he shut the door behind him, dropped his bag, and exhaled for the first time since the woods.

The stillness hit like a wave.

He crossed to the living room, opened his laptop, and began scanning. No messages from his New York team. One flagged file from the London office, a deadline that had already expired.

He ignored it.

His mind drifted with the knowledge that normalcy was no longer a given.

Chapter 8:
CASSIE REEVE

Langley's sub-level 4 didn't run on clocks.

The rooms were soundless, sterile, matte-lit to flatten time itself; time here was irrelevant. Threat didn't keep office hours.

Cassie wore severity like others wore comfort. Dark hair pulled back without compromise; jacket cut sharp. Her only concession to sentiment: a battered military watch, its face scratched into constellations. When she entered a room, the room behaved.

The HVAC's low thrum hovered just high enough in the register to be noticed. She never looked at the vent. She kept her eyes on the map. The watch ticked, steady, a rhythm that had walked her out of memories more than once.

She sat at the head of the briefing table, flanked by analysts and technical liaisons from three divisions. Her fingers never moved, but the tempo of the room matched her silence.

"We've logged five geographically distinct anomaly events," said a gray-suited man from Technical Surveillance. "Hampshire, UK. Paris. Moscow. Suburban Beijing. And most recently, the Hamptons."

He tapped a control. Three soft pulses appeared on the overhead map, thermal spikes. Not identical, but resonant enough to unsettle.

"What are we seeing?" Reeve asked.

"Atmospheric deformation. Power distortion. Pulse timings are irregular. Nothing in NATO's inventory, nothing from civilian labs."

Cassie nodded once. "And the personnel?"

"Hampshire gives us the best frame. Group of nine, mostly British, male-dominated. All late twenties to early thirties. Pre-incident behavior was normal. Post-incident: group intact, reassembled in London, maintaining face-to-face contact."

He pulled up a grid of surveillance stills. Five men are shown entering a converted flat in Islington.

"That's their central site, owned by Thomas Albright. But what matters isn't the group activity. It's the follow-up."

"Go on," Cassie said.

"They meet as a unit weekly. But each has been observed meeting one-on-one elsewhere, with him."

He enlarged a still: Jude Black, collar turned up, leaving a café.

"Meetings are irregular, non-social, and always off-comm. He initiates them."

"So he's not just part of the group," Reeve said. "He's managing it."

"It tracks. His digital history is clean, but the noise is too precise. Education, finance, relocation. Everything scans... too well."

Cassie didn't respond. Another analyst leaned forward.

"We've flagged activity linked to the Hamptons event. Subject: Congresswoman Jennifer Graves. Elected fourteen months ago. Recently, her voting patterns have shifted with more proactive national security stances, especially on aerospace threat detection and data retention. She just landed a slot on the subcommittee for defense intel oversight."

"And the link?" Cassie asked.

"Two anomalies: One, her district's comm logs show satellite interference identical to Hampshire. Two, since her committee placement, she's requested four classified briefings: orbital anomaly tracking, high-altitude unregistered activity, and non-state signal interference. All well outside her legislative scope."

Reeve's eyes narrowed. "And Beijing?"

"No identified personnel yet. Signals originated near the Zhongnanhai perimeter. PLA locked down chatter. We're blind without a leak."

Cassie stood.

"I want deeper surveillance on all nine from Hampshire. Passive only. Extend to their contacts, especially Black. Track behavioral drift. If he's a conductor, I want to know the song."

Later, Reeve stood with David North, her deputy, in a soundproof cube off the corridor.

The wall screen showed Jude Black walking the South Bank, coat shifting in the river breeze. His posture was easy. His eyes weren't.

"You think he's running them?" North asked.

"Yes."

"Or do they think he is?"

Reeve let silence work. Then: "Either way, I want to know why they're listening."

Her arms folded as she watched Jude stroll through a London square on the live feed.

He moved with the calm of someone who knew how to be invisible.

"Still no direct indicators," David North said, stepping beside her. "All chatter from Thomas' flat scans as social. But frequency's high, and the contact patterns... they're off."

"Define off."

"Too orchestrated. Like they're keeping time to a rhythm no one else hears."

Reeve tapped the screen, flipping through stills: Tom, Leo, Adeel, Mike, Nate. Each was caught separately over the past month. Always arriving alone. Always leaving together.

"And Graves?"

"Still clean in public. But off-comm most nights. Staff shunts her digital through a private relay. We're tracing."

Reeve stepped back from the wall.

"It's not enough."

"Meaning?"

"Meaning we don't have confirmation. But we have rhythm, and rhythm is the start of a pattern. I want someone watching the pattern."

She keyed a short burst into a terminal marked 'D3 – Reserved'.

North glanced at her as the feeds dimmed.

"What if it's nothing?"

"Then he disappears, and no one remembers."

"And if it's something?"

She stared at Jude's frozen image. A quiet man holding nothing.

"Then we might already be late."

In a quiet apartment in Silver Spring, Maryland, a man read a single-line message on a decommissioned secure device:

Initiate quiet contact. Flagged group. Hampshire anomaly thread.

No further instructions. He didn't need them.

Early forties. Ex–special operations turned analyst. Known only as Marsten.

He stood from his desk, closed a thin black laptop, and reached for the coat he hadn't worn in four years.

A couple of days later, he landed in London under a transit alias that didn't match the passport in his coat.

No checked bag. Just a carry-on briefcase and a tablet no one else could unlock.

By his second morning, Marsten had already mapped Jude Black's routes: the walk from flat to office, the gym rotation, the café he never entered but always passed. Patterns.

Except the pattern didn't hold.

Twice, Jude detoured down streets that weren't on his calendar. Once, he paused at a bench near a monument he never looked at. He never smiled. Never checked his phone.

It wasn't sloppy. It was too smooth.

Marsten filed five sentences in his first report:

Target operates within urban camouflage. Displays civilian rhythm with zero signal noise. No anxiety tells and no touchpoint drift. Conclusion: improbable normalcy. Recommend sustained observation.

Later that night, Cassie read the report in her Georgetown apartment. The walls were lined with hardcovers she hadn't opened in years; foreign policy first editions, intelligence memoirs, and a handful of philosophy texts worn from her undergraduate days.

She didn't sit while reading. She paced. Always had.

Her mind drifted back to Syria.

That day, the dust didn't fall. It hung, turning noon the color of old teeth, making distance theoretical. The generator's hum carried half a note wrong, just enough to itch at the edge of hearing. Cassie checked it twice. No one else noticed.

Leila, the clinic medic, handed her gauze. You're listening for a thing that won't introduce itself, she'd said.

Cassie walked the perimeter anyway. Their routine: clap once near the fence, count the seconds until the echo came back.

That day, the echo never returned.

She logged it: 12:07, no echo.

Outside the wall, a white truck idled closer than before. Not movement, intent. Four men are in the bed. One wore a scarf that didn't belong, and a watch too clean. She couldn't see the device. Only the space where it should be.

"It's not a checkpoint," she told Leila.

"What is it then?"

"An ending."

Cassie raised the radio, using a name she wasn't supposed to speak on open channels. The voice that answered was gravel and certainty: "South road compromised. West field in thirty. Keep your head down."

She did neither.

The blast took the windows first, the overpressure that made glass into teeth. The truck never touched the clinic wall, but its intent did. Two civilians, one armed. Evacuation through the west field.

Later, the report wanted boxes ticked. She wrote: Casualties confirmed. Evac successful.

What she didn't write: the dog's belated bark, the taste of powdered glass, the way Leila's hand left her shoulder and didn't return.

Years afterward, a kettle's whistle could still tighten her chest. She always counted to nine. On ten, the truck had shifted. On eleven, the world did.

She kept the watch. She learned to hear the half-note.

The floors creaked in certain spots, the only things in the apartment allowed to make noise. The radiator hissed now and then, like it had something to say about the past.

She walked barefoot over the cool wooden planks, a mug of untouched tea cooling on the sideboard. In the corner hung a wall-mounted map of Eurasia, not decoration, but marked in her own hand with pencil lines and notes from a case three years old. She hadn't erased them.

Her phone buzzed twice. Ignored.

A terminal flashed with Department chatter. Also ignored.

She reread Marsten's five lines and circled *improbable*. The word offended her. Probability was what people reached for when they ran out of discipline. She underlined it until the paper thinned, then set the pen down, closed her eyes, and listened for the half-note in the apartment's hum.

It wasn't there. It would be, soon enough.

Cassie stepped toward the window. The air smelled faintly of old paper and lemon cleaner, the kind of scent that told you someone was trying to keep time at bay.

She didn't see the Potomac anymore when she looked out. She saw trajectories, the paths things took when no one paid attention. The noise most people filtered out.

When she was a child, she had watched her mother count down seconds before the kettle boiled and had learned two things:

First, that small events could be predicted.

Second, that if you missed enough of them, something always boiled over.

Her mother had died from an infection that no one caught in time. Her first field operation ended with two analysts dead because a diplomat "didn't seem suspicious."

So Cassie stopped trusting feelings.

She trusted disturbance.

Jude Black was a disturbance wearing a suit.

And if she didn't follow it, no one would.

Elsewhere, dawn arrived in Sag Harbor with the civility of a metronome. The estate had too many windows and not enough corners, which suited her fine. Corners taught people to think defensively.

Nireva stood barefoot on the cold stone, the host body's skin prickling in protest she declined to register. The woman's name, Jennifer Graves, fit neatly in rooms that required it. The mouth shaped consensus well. Blonde hair, blue eyes: a vanity she had not chosen, but one she would use.

"Congresswoman," said her chief of staff from the doorway, holding a folder like a sacrament. "Revised remarks for the oversight breakfast."

She didn't turn.

"Strike the verbs that apologize," she said. "Keep the nouns that frighten without proof."

A beat. "And the ask?"

"Data continuity authority. Quiet sunset clauses. You will bury the leverage where patriots forget to look."

He hesitated at the phrasing—too sharp, too clean—then retreated to soften it for the people who would hear it.

She watched three gulls argue like failed diplomats and thought of an Aethero warrior she was once close with, engine and edge, calling force a strategy. He would test the wire until it cut him. He always had. She had trusted him once the way you trust a locked door: useful, until you need to leave.

Vael was more interesting. He built rooms inside rooms and invited people to call it architecture. She aligned with him when it suited the mission, and left when the mission changed. He mistook that for disloyalty. Males with plans often did.

Her phone chimed with the kind of message that pretended to be an accident; syntax too careful, intent too clean.

Almost right. Grammar is almost wrong. She smiled. Someone was fishing with broken glyphs. Someone wanted to see who could still read.

"Trace?" she asked without moving.

"Non-attributed," the staffer said from the hall. "But the routing is playful."

"Then play," she said. "Two steps. No more."

In a few hours, she would sit before a table of men who had already decided to be convinced, and offer them sentences cut to their appetite. She would let them believe the phrase threat envelope had been theirs. She would secure another small law that added up to a large silence.

Later, she would dress the host precisely: navy that read as steel, the silver pin, the half-smile. She would take the long car to the city where money bruised the air and say the word oversight until it stopped meaning anything at all.

There was a photo on the desk in the study, Graves with the donor whose estate she now used as a staging ground. He was smiling with his entire face. She touched the glass because the host would have; mourning is a social vector, and she preferred not to waste it.

The ocean kept its manners. The house kept its secrets. She kept her options.

"Schedule a call with Defense," she said. "There's a new vector in play. Shadow, not signal. Track it."

She passed the mirror and let the host see herself: the immaculate line, the posture that promised order, the eyes that performed warmth. Nireva noted the performance and approved. Humanity loved a mask that smiled while it measured.

On the drive in, she composed a sentence designed to be quoted and misremembered. By the time the first reporter tweeted it, she had already built the next room.

Chapter 9: QUIET ONES

Six months had passed since the Hampshire incident, and the world had continued to turn.

Jude Black now moved through his life with the kind of precision that made him look ordinary. Weekdays belonged to Mayfair and Canary Wharf boardrooms, where he managed portfolios and asset exits. Evenings went to dinners with clients, check-ins with his mother, calls with his father's aide about local media optics, and the occasional quiet hour with his sister in Fitzrovia where they traded barbs about everything except the truth.

The truth had relocated to a different level.

Each of his five closest friends, or what remained of them, had begun applying themselves with calculated intent. The Aethero, despite their alien origin, had learned quickly that Earth's systems ran on language, influence, and information.

Leo—Skael—had embedded himself deeper into consulting networks, positioning for access to multinationals operating across sectors.

Nate, carrying Rakkar, worked his way through London's venture tech scene, showing up at AI panels and machine ethics roundtables.

Kareth, in Mike's body, had taken quiet contract work in data systems; surveillance-adjacent, always observing.

Tom, inhabited by Zherin, leveraged his architecture portfolio to join urban redevelopment boards; a slow game, but a patient one.

And Adeel, once known for his charm and courtroom precision, now, as Sarun, moved like a shadow in regulatory law, tracking policy drafts before even ministers saw them.

They met regularly, always at Tom's flat, always under the guise of "old friends catching up." No digital trace. No photos. No paper.

And always, after those meetings, Jude saw each of them again over the ensuing days. Separately.

He gave them different instructions each time.

Not because he didn't trust them—though he never truly did. But because he needed to know who would break formation first.

Five months ago

Tom-Zherin's apartment sat between a minimalist storefront and a wine bar in Clerkenwell. High ceilings. Matte steel accents. The indie vibe long since drained from the air.

Jude stood by the window, watching the late afternoon light spill across the street below. Five of them were present, all men. The women had been told this was "just work stuff." They hadn't questioned it.

The others stood in a loose arc: Mike-Kareth, Nate-Rakkar, Leo-Skael, Adeel-Sarun, and Tom-Zherin himself. Each wore their host with growing confidence. Their mannerisms had sharpened, their cadence more convincingly human. By the third day, they were almost flawless.

Jude felt the weight of Vael's presence pressing from within.

"They expect clarity," Vael said.

"Then let them expect it," Jude replied. *"And receive something else."*

Mike-Kareth broke the silence first.

"We've been waiting."

Jude nodded. "Good. You're adapting quickly."

Tom-Zherin tilted his head. "We expected a more advanced operational sequence by now. The host environment is ready for infiltration."

"And that's why we don't move quickly," Jude said.

Leo-Skael frowned. "Explain."

Jude turned from the window.

"This world doesn't react to force. It absorbs it. Pressure creates resistance. Move too fast, and it notices. Act like a threat, and it raises defenses. Human systems may be slow, but they are reflexive."

"That's not what our protocols anticipated," Adeel-Sarun said.

"The protocols were built on incomplete variables, and our intelligence was forty years old," Jude replied. "We're not just observing. We're embedding. Subtlety wins."

"You sound like me," Vael murmured.

"You would have come in like a blade," Jude thought. *"I prefer the needle."*

He stepped toward Nate-Rakkar.

"You'll begin monitoring the other scout teams. I want their current positioning, behavioral shifts, and operational pace."

"Should I liaise with them?" Nate-Rakkar asked.

"No. You report only to me. Secure channel. No noise."

Nate-Rakkar nodded. No resistance.

Tom-Zherin spoke. "Do we guide infrastructure manipulation?"

Jude searched for glimpses of the old friend he once knew.

"Not yet. Influence must be masked through human channels. We push only where their systems expect human ambition."

"What if another cell moves ahead?"

Jude let the silence stretch.

"Then we absorb the consequences, or we absorb the cell."

Leo-Skael glanced up at that, a flicker of tension crossing his face.

Jude pressed on.

"Our crash site was chosen for a reason. That building frequently hosts off-grid retreats for influential figures from the UK, US, and Europe—ministers, economists, scientists, security leaders. We were meant to embed near power. But we ended up in bodies much younger than expected, with uncertain social leverage. That makes speed our enemy. Move too fast, and we lose the illusion."

Kareth stayed silent.

Jude met his eyes briefly.

"He's waiting," Vael said. *"For a mistake. For deviation."*

"Let him keep waiting," Jude replied.

The meeting dissolved on cue. No orders were given; they simply understood when it was over.

Jude lingered after the door shut.

Tom-Zherin stood in the doorway.

"You speak like a host who never yielded."

Jude smiled thinly.

"I speak like a general who understands exactly what's at stake. I'm your Takra for a reason."

Tom-Zherin's eyes lingered a moment too long.

Then: "Acknowledged."

He retreated into the next room. The door clicked behind him.

Jude exhaled, slow and silent. With Tom-Zherin, it was different. Their friendship had once been real; boarding school years, long weekends in the Alps, stupid bets over coffee. Now, Jude found himself watching the curve of Tom-Zherin's smile, the way he leaned on the table, the phrasing of his jokes. He wasn't looking for mistakes. He was listening for echoes.

"*You are building something,*" Vael said, pulling Jude out of his trance.

"*No,*" Jude replied. "*I'm repurposing something you broke.*"

Present day

The intercom buzzed twice, short, deliberate.

Jude answered, then waited at the door.

Nate-Rakkar arrived minutes later, face calm, coat zipped high. He gave a brief nod and set a hard drive on the table. Jude waved him inside and locked the door behind them.

The flat was dim, lit only by the kitchen pendant. Its glow stretched across the marble island in long reflections. Beyond the glass, London blurred into a smear of rain and windows.

"Anyone see you?" Jude asked.

"One civilian at the corner shop. No tail. Not theirs, anyway."

Jude didn't ask who they were. He already knew.

He connected the drive and watched the decryption cycle spin. Glyphs bloomed, shifted, and stabilized.

Nate-Rakkar sat across from him, the hum of Jude's encrypted terminal filling the silence.

"Two scout cells confirmed," Nate-Rakkar said, sliding over a smaller drive. "One dormant. One not."

Jude plugged it in, letting the data surface.

"Locations?"

"Dormant cell's in Shanghai, seems to have shifted from Beijing. Probably a fallback or partial failure. But the active one..."

He opened his laptop, tapped a few keys, and turned the screen toward Jude.

The image filled it.

Jennifer Graves stood mid-speech at a policy summit. Mid-forties, composed, steely-eyed, immaculate. A tailored navy dress. A silver pin at her lapel. Her hand raised mid-gesture, eyes sharp, smile sharpened to political perfection. She didn't just look powerful, she looked chosen.

Nate-Rakkar let the silence stretch, then said:

"It's Nireva,"

Jude said nothing.

The pause was quiet, but not empty.

Inside, Vael surged.

"Nireva… still radiant. She never settled for ordinary hosts. She wore that body like it was forged for her. She never liked mess. Always playing angles I didn't see coming."

His tone was unreadable. Not warm. Not cold. Just… distant.

"You know her," Jude said flatly.

"She was once bonded to me," Vael replied. *"Briefly. Strategically."*

A pause.

"Then she aligned with Kareth. Briefly."

Jude raised an eyebrow at that.

"She never respected his force," Vael added quickly. *"He mistook her loyalty for affection. She let him."*

Jude leaned slightly toward Nate-Rakkar.

"She's in the Hamptons?"

"Long Island coast," Nate-Rakkar said. "Her base of operations looks like an estate she 'inherited' from a former donor. She holds a U.S. congressional seat and secured defense oversight committee access."

"She's moving fast," Jude muttered.

"She always did," Vael said. *"Unlike Kareth, she understands soft power."*

"Will she sense you're not really in control?" Jude asked.

"If your mimicry falters, yes. But she was never loyal to personality, only to vision. If she sees strength, she'll obey. If she sees doubt..."

"She'll strike," Jude finished.

"And not just with steel," Vael murmured. *"With consensus."*

Jude flipped back through the drive contents. One transmission stood out, a partial handshake ping routed through a human satellite.

"They're baiting," Jude said. "Another clan?"

"Most likely testing who else survived," Nate-Rakkar replied.

Jude allowed himself the faintest smile.

"Then bait them back. Let's see which of our dear cousins is fishing in our pond."

Nate-Rakkar loaded a broken glyph into his private system, a ping coded to read like failed protocol. Muddled syntax. Intentionally corrupted command structure. He turned his laptop to Jude.

Jude nodded.

"Push this back through the same satellite. Scrub the trail twice. I want to see who nibbles."

Nate-Rakkar hit send.

Somewhere, on another device, someone would see it and bite.

Before Nate-Rakkar left, he hesitated at the door.

"I assume you know this already... but we've been flagged."

Jude looked up.

"Who?"

"GCHQ, MI5, maybe a few desks in Langley. They've picked up on the atmospheric ripples from the crash site. And someone's built a proximity log. Your name's on it. So are mine, and the others."

Jude said nothing.

"So if we're playing slow, we'd better play quiet."

"Agreed," Jude said.

"And if we're playing quiet," Nate-Rakkar added, "we'll need to start deciding who stays visible."

Jude closed the door behind him.

Jude met Ella on a rooftop bar in Shoreditch neither of them particularly liked. She had chosen it for the view. He agreed for the distance.

The city stretched beneath them like circuitry—glass, light, movement. A city pretending not to watch itself.

Ella approached in a dark coat, hair pinned back, posture loose but eyes focused. She scanned the skyline first, then him.

"You've changed," she said, easing into the seat across from him.

"The city'll do that."

"No," she said. "I mean, since Hampshire."

She didn't say it like a question.

"You've been slow on replies," she added. "All of you, really. But you especially, to me."

The waiter came and went. She ordered wine. He didn't.

"You know," she said, swirling the glass lightly, "my minister mentioned your name a few times lately. Says you're popping up in conversations you were never in before."

Jude raised an eyebrow. "Still pretending I'm useful?"

"He said you're interesting. Which is worse."

Jude let a small smile curl at the corner of his mouth.

"We go back. My dad and his Cabinet days."

"I heard," she said. "That trip to Croatia when we were teenagers? I heard you barely spoke to anyone except your notebook."

"It wasn't a notebook," Jude said. "It was leverage."

That made her laugh, the quick, surprised kind. Her eyes softened, just for a second.

Then the moment passed.

"You're performing again."

"Always am."

"Not like this." She leaned in slightly. "Before, you performed for people. Now it's for something. Something that's watching."

Their fingers touched as he passed her the wine menu. Neither acknowledged it, but neither pulled away fast enough either.

"Maybe I'm just more serious these days," he said.

"No," she replied. "You're more committed. And that's not always the same thing as serious."

A gust of wind lifted the edge of her coat. She wrapped it tighter but didn't break eye contact.

"Whatever this is, Jude, you're not the only one watching."

"Meaning?"

"Meaning you've changed your orbit. And others are starting to notice the gravity shift."

She stood, unfinished wine in her hand, eyes still on him.

"This is me trusting you. But it's not a blank cheque."

"You think I've lost control?"

"I think you've decided it's worth the risk."

She pulled her coat back on, turned, then paused.

"You owe me clarity. And I'll collect."

And then, quieter, almost reflexive:

"You were always better when you were scared of yourself."

She left.

Jude stared at the empty chair for a long moment.

"She's sharper than most of your kind," Vael said.

"She reminds me of me," Jude replied.

"Then don't let her get too close."

"That's not up to me," Jude murmured. *"Not entirely."*

Tom-Zherin's flat was low-lit and curated to look like comfort: soft shadows, scotch on the table, windows half open to the chill. But inside, the air had an edge.

Jude entered last. The others were already there; Kareth leaning against a shelf, Tom-Zherin staring at his phone without reading it, Adeel-Sarun on the floor beside a blank legal pad. Leo-Skael stood near the kitchen, arms crossed. Nate-Rakkar sat at his laptop.

Kareth occupied the armchair, posture perfect, eyes fixed on the glass in his hand.

"Takra Vael," he said as Jude entered. A greeting. A test.

Jude nodded once. "Reports?"

"Stability," Adeel-Sarun said. "No significant shifts in legislation. Access remains discreet."

"Urban planning approvals move forward without resistance," Tom-Zherin reported. "I've begun shaping influence toward key sites. We should be able to secure a strong location for the reconnaissance phase."

"Signal scanning through consultancy channels continues," Leo-Skael said. "Nothing unexpected."

Kareth waited for the others to finish. Then: "And the other clans?"

"Nireva is consolidating power," Jude replied. "The Hamptons cell is operating as predicted. No contact initiated."

"That's the point," Kareth said. "No contact. No coordination. You've withheld alignment with Nireva."

Jude studied him. "You think I should open communication?"

"She was seeded for a reason. She's already on the defense oversight subcommittee. She's signaling."

"And I'm watching."

Kareth set his glass down with deliberate weight. "You delay. You maneuver. But this isn't *vel'taren*. We are not meant to linger in shad ow."

The phrase landed heavy, formal. Ancient.

"He's baiting you," Vael whispered inside.

"Noted," Jude thought.

"Don't answer like prey."

Jude moved to the counter, resting his hands lightly on its edge.

"No," he said aloud. "We're meant to win. And for that, we must move at the pace of the skin we wear."

Kareth stepped forward, just enough to tilt the room's balance.

"You sound like someone who's begun to wear the host too comfortably."

Jude's jaw tightened. He forced the tension down his spine.

"No, Kareth. I've simply learned to weaponize it."

Silence. Kareth studied him, really studied, as though calculating which variables he'd missed.

At last: "Then may your path remain *vel'saan.*" *Survivable.*

The word wasn't for Jude.

It was for the room.

A signal, not of loyalty, but of patience worn thin. An invitation disguised as respect.

Then Kareth turned and walked out, not waiting to be dismissed.

The door clicked closed.

The others lingered, uneasy. Tom-Zherin left next, into his room, muttering about an early start. Leo-Skael followed, then Adeel-Sarun. Nate-Rakkar gave Jude a long, measuring look before stepping out last.

Silence settled in the flat like dust.

Vael's voice stirred, quieter now. Less mocking. More curious.

"That's the tone his brother used. Before his insubordination trial."

Jude didn't move.

"What happened?" he asked.

"He argued too often. Subtly. Precisely. Until the wrong person listened. He was removed."

"And Kareth?"

"Learned to wait longer before drawing his blade."

Jude poured himself a drink and let the scotch burn its way down.

"Kareth's waiting for someone to make a mistake."

"Then don't make one."

Back in his flat, Jude stared across the city, lit by sodium fog and red aircraft warnings. London was always quietest just before 4 a.m., the hour of second thoughts.

He didn't sleep much anymore. Not because he couldn't, but because he might miss something.

The table behind him glowed with open files. No paper, digital only. Layers of mapped influence, glyph intercepts, and behavioral pattern analysis.

He turned to his secure terminal. The glyphic ping he'd sent days earlier had received no direct reply, but there had been a ripple.

One of the scout clusters, one Jude hadn't expected to activate, had adjusted its comm signature.

Too subtle for anyone else to notice.

But not for him.

"They moved," he said aloud.

"Nireva's network?" Vael asked.

"No. China. Slight shift in frequency. Suggests they're listening, but not responding. Not yet."

Then we provoke. Strategically.

Jude nodded.

"We're going to break the symmetry."

He opened a new draft, not a message, but an organizational framework. One he'd been sketching in secret, away from the others. It didn't use Earth terminology or Aethero military rank.

It was a third structure. A hybrid. Built around decision autonomy, trust gradients, and segmented intelligence. A system that didn't demand loyalty, but rewarded outcome.

"You're dividing them," Vael said. Not disapproving. Just observing.

"Not yet," Jude replied. *"I'm giving them gravity. One by one. So when the division comes, it won't feel like fracture."*

Clever.

"Necessary."

He paused, then added quietly: *"If I wait for them to turn, I lose initiative. If I turn them first, I gain their shape."*

Vael was silent for a long moment. Then:

"You were never just a host, were you?"

"No," Jude said. *"I was always the cage."*

Chapter 10: FAULT LINES

Eight months since the Hampshire incident

The report arrived at 07:12 GMT.

Cassie read it twice before setting her coffee down. The white ceramic cup clicked against the steel tabletop, the sound sharper than it should have been in the quiet of Langley's sub-briefing annex. She leaned forward, eyes narrowing on the key lines—Marsten's clipped, meticulous field notes, written in his usual dry cadence.

Subject J. Black has resumed patterns of 'civilian engagement' after twenty days of minimal movement. Two meetings outside routine, both unannounced; one with E. Meyer (Government aide, MoD adjoint), one with an unidentified male, possibly academic. Facial recognition pending. Behavior suggests reconnaissance or message distribution.

Cassie tapped her pen against the page. This was the second deviation in six weeks. The team had initially flagged Jude's return from Hampshire as coinciding with several anomalies, but now the pattern shifted from passive reconstruction to something more deliberate.

She opened a secure channel to Marsten.

"Surveillance upgrade authorized," she said. "Passive observation of the other five males. Start with Nate, the tech guy."

"Understood," Marsten replied. "We'll run mobile stingrays where signal bleed permits. Do you want routine interception on Meyer as well?"

"Not yet. She's connected, and they may be monitoring for that."

A pause.

"You're expecting a leak?"

Cassie exhaled slowly. "No. I'm expecting a test."

She ended the call and leaned back in her chair. Outside the soundproofed glass, the corridor pulsed with idle footsteps and recycled air.

Her eyes drifted to the corkboard on the far wall. A photo, half-buried under notes and satellite shots, caught her attention.

Young Cassie. Hair pulled into a tight braid. Desert heat in her smile. Laughing beside a woman from a unit she hadn't spoken to in years. Damascus. Before this job. Before the clean suits and optical taps. Before the paranoia became routine.

She let the memory hold her a moment longer, then turned back to the tablet.

Jude Black was moving again.

And this time, she was going to follow every step.

The Mayfair office smelled faintly of cedar, marble polish, and ambition.

Jude sat at the edge of the conference table, one leg crossed, hands resting lightly over a briefing folder. The document inside had nothing to do with finance. It was a refined legal insert, seven pages of perfectly phrased ambiguity, ready to be slipped into the stack of policy amendments awaiting an aide at the Ministry of Defence.

Adeel-Sarun sat opposite, unusually still.

"You're sure this won't cause blowback?" he asked.

"It's just language," Jude said. "Flexible, deniable, buried. If they're watching, it's not us they'll see. It's their own machinery stumbling."

Adeel-Sarun nodded slowly. "And if they trace it?"

"Then we'll know who's looking."

When Adeel-Sarun left, Jude spoke again—not aloud, but inward, to the presence that had been listening since dawn.

"You disapprove."

"It is not disapproval," Vael replied, his voice cool in the white expanse. *"It is timing. You are inviting observation prematurely."*

"A pattern that doesn't shift," Jude murmured, *"is easier to detect."*

"That is the logic of a saboteur, not a strategist."

"Sometimes they're the same thing."

Silence stretched between them, not combative but taut. Jude had learned to treat Vael's silences as the truest measure of his reactions. Stillness meant concern. Argument meant comfort.

Back in the real world, Jude tapped the folder once, then slid it into his briefcase. He stood, adjusted his cuffs, and left the conference room, descending by private lift to the side entrance of the building.

The sky was cold; London grey, vaguely wet, always listening.

He took the long route to his car, passing pavement cafés and men in coats pretending they weren't watching. One of them might be Marsten, the name Nate-Rakkar had flagged. The glance was too casual, the umbrella too dry.

The warehouse was silent except for the low hum of generators beneath the floor.

Outside, rusted rail lines stretched into nothing, relics no one had touched in years. Inside, soft industrial light pooled across the concrete, casting long shadows over crates that hadn't been moved in a decade. It was the kind of place no one asked questions about, where plans were whispered, not written. A hidden site, secured by them.

Kareth stood at the center, arms crossed, eyes half-shadowed beneath the skylights. Tom and Leo faced him, or rather, Zherin and Skael, the minds within them. Their human faces were expressionless, their stillness perfected over months, almost unnerving.

"He is not the same," Kareth said. "Vael would never withhold tactical contact this long. He would never stall network assembly. He would never cede the initiative to uncertainty."

"The human world is not ours," Leo-Skael replied. "Adaptation was expected."

"Adaptation, yes," Kareth snapped. "Infiltration. Not stagnation. What you call adaptation smells of doubt."

Tom-Zherin tilted his head. "And if you're wrong? If this is Vael's method? Calculated patience? He is our Takra for a reason."

"Then let him explain it. Face to face," Kareth said, stepping forward. "He won't, because it's not him. The host is stronger than expected. His will has corrupted Vael's clarity."

A pause settled. Dust drifted in the shafts of light like static.

"I've found something," Kareth continued, lower now. "From the old briefings. Legacy instructions embedded in the Phase One relay. There's a signal array, buried, old-world tech, still responsive. In France. If we activate it..."

"That wasn't authorized," Tom-Zherin said.

"It wasn't forbidden," Kareth answered.

Leo-Skael glanced between them. For a moment, it was just three bodies in a dead room, but beneath the silence, something sharp shifted. Friction. Doubt. Power unspoken.

"You want a coup," Leo-Skael said finally.

"I want a return," Kareth replied. "To the Aethero we were before this world infected our thinking."

Tom-Zherin didn't speak.

But he didn't leave either.

The expanse

They stood again in the white.

Not summoned. Not called. Simply there, as if thought itself had rippled outward and folded reality around them. The endless expanse stretched in every direction: no sky, floor, or gravity. Just light without a source.

Jude stood with his hands in his pockets. Vael, still in his dark form, circled the edges of their invisible center.

"Kareth has always confused purity with strength," Vael said.

Jude didn't answer. He watched the glimmer of nothing shift under his feet, like mist across glass.

"Do you believe he's wrong?" he asked at last.

"No," Vael replied. *"But I believe he's unfinished."*

"He believes you are."

Vael stopped moving.

"He wants to return to the original infiltration plan," Jude continued. *"But I don't think you even want that anymore."*

A flicker passed through Vael's form; static, brief, and brittle. Not fear. Not anger. Uncertainty.

"What I want," Vael said slowly, *"no longer fits into the words I knew."*

Jude turned toward him, calm, cold.

"Good. That means you're thinking."

Silence stretched. Not empty. Heavy, thick with things unsaid.

"And if Kareth acts?" Jude asked.

"Then he will fail," Vael said. *"Because he underestimates the human, he believes me too weak to control."*

Jude smiled, faintly.

"Then let's give him something to choke on."

Vael's image dissolved.

Jude let his mind settle, remembering words Vael had spoken months before, when the cage was new, and the balance between them less certain.

Five pods. Five clans of the Aethero.

That was the shape of it. Not conquest, not yet. Preparation. Finance, politics, intelligence, energy, arms. Each pod seeded to worm its way into the arteries of Earth's power. By the time the fleet arrived, governments and institutions would already be compromised. Earth wouldn't need to be taken by fire; its doors would be opened from within.

He remembered the pause in Vael's voice, the rare hesitation. The plan had been built from stolen Xanathi Assembly Archives intelligence frozen in the 1990s. A world mapped as it had been, not as it was now.

Vael had admitted it quietly: the strategy was clumsy, improvised. A scaffolding raised in haste. A half-measure against the High Circle's original intent for a full fleet invasion to seize land for their people. The pods relied on untested technology; proof-of-concept devices able to absorb and transfer consciousness, smuggled across the galaxy in silence.

Jude turned the memory like a coin. That was the irony. The Aethero believed themselves prepared, but their preparation was already out of date. Their fleet still crawled along the Assembly's back roads, years away. And in the meantime, here on Earth, Jude was the one adapting.

PART III:

POWER SHADOWS

Chapter 11:
PARIS STING

Ten months since the Hampshire incident

The signal wasn't a message so much as an imprint—a pattern impressed on a commercial satellite's maintenance ping, a ghost handshake riding the heartbeat of a French-owned relay. It looked like static until it didn't. Rakkar froze it frame by frame and peeled back the checksum the way a watchmaker lifts a faceplate.

"There," Rakkar said, tapping the glitching edge of a subroutine. "Not human code. The grammar's wrong. It's... copied from something, but the order isn't ours."

Jude leaned over his shoulder. The glyph cadence was unmistakable, even when it pretended to be broken. A cousin clan's musicality, close enough to his ear now that he could tell them apart. He'd taught himself to do that. You never leave the primitive tool lying around if you can turn it into a scalpel.

He had Rakkar run a differential against the bait glyph they'd pushed a few months earlier. The overlap was just enough to make Jude's lips crease.

"They bit," Jude said.

Rakkar zoomed the map. The return trace hopped from Brest to Limoges and then jittered toward Paris, like someone testing towers as they moved, piggybacking on civic infrastructure; clean routing, awkward timing. Amateur-professional. Aethero wearing a human watch.

"Paris," Rakkar said. "Seventeenth or Eighth, judging by the bounce. Maybe they're keeping to ring roads."

"The Paris pod," Jude murmured. "They made it."

He didn't say I drew them. He didn't need to.

In the white expanse, memory played itself in perfect fidelity. *"Five pods; five clans,"* Vael had said. *"France is one of them; assembly, defense, Europe's spine."* Pride under the words, and something else: the old certainty that plans were good because they were his.

Jude blinked, and the expanse went dark. London returned, clean glass, a skyline that never slept. He touched the window once, as if to ground himself, and said: "Book Paris."

Rakkar said, "When?"

"Now."

Night was a thin fog pressed to the Potomac, sodium gold over black water. Cassie Reeve stood at the window and let the river fall away until it was just trajectories again, lines crossing lines, saying more in silence than they ever did in speech.

On her desk, the DGSI liaison had left a polite email wrapped in three layers of French formality: *We're seeing anomalies through a private satellite. Low likelihood. Happy to brief if you're in town.* That had been eight hours ago. Since then, the anomalies had grown teeth.

David dropped a printout on her desk. "Paris. Seventeenth. Travel agency front that's never sold a ticket. And the bank accounts? Rented servers in Belgium, paid in cash by a man who doesn't exist."

Cassie skimmed the highlights and stopped on the packet loss graph. The artifact pattern was familiar, a hand she'd felt brushing past her in three different cities over six months. Whoever they were, they had a style.

"Book the team," she said.

"Legal wants us to coordinate with DGSI."

"We'll coordinate. We just won't wait. Tell Marsten to fly out too."

He nodded. They'd done this dance before. She'd cut her teeth running agents across the Syrian border, timing raids to the minute so a city wouldn't realize an artery had been cut until the patient was already dead. Paris was different in all the ways that mattered and none of the ones that counted. Systems were systems. People bled the same.

She closed her eyes on the plane and let training run beneath consciousness like a tide. The Stingray rigs would hide inside an unmarked van. Micro-drones packed in foam would ride in a line technician's satchel. Marsten would sit two blocks away with a cup of coffee and look like he belonged. The rest would be silence until it wasn't.

Her mind drifted to Jude, *"Somehow he's connected to this."*

Paris knew how to be damp in ways other cities forgot. The patina on stone, the slickness on a painted door, the faint smell of leaves and smoke. Kareth walked as if the pavement owed him something; fast, too fast, the new coat stiff over his shoulders, the bad shave raising angry red along his jaw.

Skael kept half a pace behind and a degree to the left, the way you do when you want to see both your partner and the street. He scanned windows, the undersides of balconies, the sudden absences on rooftops where there should have been clutter, and wasn't. He liked Paris well enough. He just didn't trust it.

"They'll listen," Kareth said, not turning his head. "Blood binds. We speak, they align."

Skael didn't answer. He'd learned the value of not answering certain sentences over the past six months. He let the city speak instead: delivery trucks, bikes, shoes, the soft hydraulic sigh of a bus kneeling.

The travel agency looked like the idea of a travel agency a child might draw from memory: faded posters of the Côte d'Azur, a model airplane yellowed in the window. They went up the back stairs and knocked three times.

Seven. That was the count as the door opened. Five men, two women. Faces chosen precisely for forgettability, the way you choose a key to match every lock. One of the women had a small white scar bridging her nose, an accident, not a battle. The scholar in the middle had good shoes and a body more used to reading than running.

"You're late," the scholar said in English because it drew a line, and he liked lines.

Kareth squared his shoulders. "Insertion was rough. These hosts were not in the best position socially. We surfaced when we could."

A small flinch ran through the room at the hosts. Even among their own, the word sat like a splinter. The scarred woman's eyes tightened.

"We were told to seed," she said in French. "To wait. To prepare the ground, not stomp holes in it."

Kareth's smile flashed too many teeth. "And yet the ground remains unprepared. Earth moves; you have not."

Skael shifted his stance. He could feel the room tipping, weight sliding to one side.

The scholar's hand slipped under the table. Not quick; deliberate. Skael's breath caught for a second.

"We answer to Vael," the scholar said. "Are you Vael? No. You are a zealot wearing his syllables. And kin to a disgraced one."

Kareth's chin lifted. "I carry Vael's mandate."

The room appeared unconvinced. Not because they preferred to listen to Vael, but rather, they had decided to operate within clan lines, and the mention of the First Regiment's Takra was just an excuse.

Skael felt the line cross in the air, an invisible thing, but you knew it when it snapped. He eased his foot back, found the angle to the corridor with the kind of practiced clumsiness that makes it look like you tripped when what you did was choose the ground.

Across the boulevard, Jude stirred his coffee without looking at it. He liked cafés before things happened. The theatre of it. Seeing people constructing their small shelters out of routine. In those moments, cities declare themselves in ways they do not during sirens.

Rakkar sat with a second laptop open, piggybacking a fraction of Cassie's drone feed he had not been invited to see. "Our boy is about to make a speech that gets him shot," he said mildly.

Jude nodded once. "He will get halfway through a sentence, someone else will finish for him with a gun."

"Do we intervene?"

"When it's useful."

Rakkar flicked a glance at the travel agency door. "Are we useful today?"

Jude smiled slightly. "We will be soon."

He had walked this block twice the week before, once with a newspaper and once with a coffee, counting cameras and the reflection angles of glass doors. Now, when he crossed the street at a time that looked careless, he was only stepping onto a line he'd already drawn.

Cassie's world was grayscale and geometry two blocks away, stitched by twelve camera angles and a packet map. The Stingray had begun its mimicry; phones came to it like moths to a brighter porchlight. She tagged seven devices moving as a flock, then lost three as they drifted. Panic will scatter you in your own head before it scatters your feet.

"Audio?" she asked.

"Thin," Marsten said in her ear. "We're bouncing off old ducts. We'll have bursts."

"Give me posture, then."

"Standing, leaning, coiled, and one about to do something ill-advised," Marsten said. He'd learned her language over five years and took pleasure in speaking it back to her.

Cassie watched the way the scholar's shoulders squared, the way the scarred woman's jaw set. The camera caught a slice of metal at the edge of the table.

"Gun," she said. "Greenlight the sting. Move."

The café emptied itself of two men who hadn't been there a moment earlier. The municipal van's hazard lights flicked twice and went dark. Someone took an apple out of a pocket and threw it in a bin, because hands like rituals before they do violence.

Cassie stood, felt the weight of the pistol and the lighter weight of certainty, and walked.

The room had the feel of an argument that had been waiting in the walls for six months and finally found people to inhabit it. Kareth refused to bring his voice down. The scholar refused to raise his. The scarred woman did not blink.

"We seed. We infiltrate. We adapt," the scholar said again, each clause a rung on a ladder. "You demand obedience, but obedience to what? Your pace? Your ego?"

"To the plan," Kareth snapped. "You starve a city while we are here to take its larder. You bow to humans as if their nets were better than your will."

"You misread the nets," the scarred woman said. "And your will is not an instrument. It is a hammer. Hammers break what we are supposed to shape."

Kareth took a step forward, and Skael took one back, not because he intended to leave but because he wanted more space for what he knew would follow.

"We were told to wait for contact," the scholar said. "So we waited. Then a cousin's voice touched the net and pulled back. That was not you."

Kareth's expression cooled. "We don't own all the air. But we are here now. You will move when we say."

"No," the scholar said simply.

The movement was small and everything: his hand completing its journey under the table, the metal rising, the room shrinking to the line drawn by a muzzle. Skael saw the trigger finger, too tight and too white; saw the woman's shoulders set; saw Kareth's jaw yank left with anger instead of down with caution.

Skael whispered, "Don't."

The door burst inward in white light and thunder.

Flashbang. A little world destroyed and remade in a heartbeat. The travel agency cracked open like an egg into sound and smoke.

Cassie's first step into the room was a memory trained into the present: left, low, sweep, identify, isolate. Her operators filled the space with speed and angles. One went high past the door, and one knelt to catch the feet of anyone who believed in miracles. Sound came back in like tide after fracture: shouting, the hollow slap of a shot into plaster, the zip of a bullet that had no line left to travel.

The scholar fired twice and hit nobody. The scarred woman stayed down and lived, because sometimes the difference between dead and alive is the choice to be smaller than your courage tells you to be. Two of the men ran for the window and didn't get there. Another got there and left blood on the glass that would be power-washed by noon.

Skael pulled Kareth without asking, because he had always known that one day he would have to carry the man who wouldn't carry himself. They hit the corridor. The first ricochet took a chunk of plaster near Kareth's ear, making him stumble. Skael shouldered him into the shadow of a copy machine that had not worked since the last government forgot to replace the toner.

Cassie cut the room into pockets and collapsed them, one after the other. Her voice stayed level on the net. "Left clear. Right, two. Corridor movement, two unknowns."

"Corridor boxed," Marsten replied. "Stairs are ours. Back door chained."

The scarred woman's weapon skittered out of reach, and she didn't try to crawl after it. She lay with her cheek to the tile, watching Cassie with a stare that had weight.

Cassie nodded once to an operator who knew how to cuff wrists without breaking them. She turned to the corridor, where the sound had changed.

"Two moving," Marsten said. "One helping the other."

"Noted," Cassie said, and felt the universe tilt the smallest degree toward whatever came next.

Kareth hit the service door at speed and lost. The chain held, the door didn't think much of him, and the world isn't obligated to open because you shout at it.

"They've boxed us," Skael said. He wasn't panicking. He was accounting.

"Then we break the box," Kareth snarled and threw his shoulder again.

"You'll die there," a third voice said.

Jude stepped into the corridor like he had been behind the door the entire time. He carried nothing. He carried everything.

Kareth stared. He had imagined a savior would look like a sword. Jude looked like a sentence that ended itself.

"How," Kareth began, because zealots ask how only when the room is already on fire.

"Later," Jude said. "Follow."

He mapped the space: old building, service spine running parallel to the retail units, electrical conduit in metal trays, maintenance crawlspaces cut by men who did not respect straight lines.

He reached for a panel whose screws anyone else would have missed because paint had pretended to cover them. The panel came away. The crawlspace smelled like dust and old breath.

"Go," Jude said.

Skael didn't argue. He shoved Kareth through and went after. Jude replaced the panel with the soft, sure movement that makes a lie convince the world to be true a few seconds longer. He waited, counted the breaths he'd allowed himself to have, then moved.

An operator reached the corridor mouth and saw nothing, just the chain on the back door and the harmless rectangle of a wall. Cassie's voice filtered in: "Back hall?"

"Negative," came the reply. "Clear."

The copy machine chose that moment to let its drum settle with a clunk that sounded like misdirection if you'd already decided to be misdirected. Two operators aimed there. Jude was already twenty feet away, ghosting down a parallel line the drones didn't see because the drones were looking where humans were supposed to be.

He ducked into the ceiling void one flight down and moved in a crouch, fingers and knees, the way you do when the building is the only ally you have. He flipped a breaker in a junction box and sent a dark square of stairwell into blindness. Above him, boots hesitated and voices misread the map.

He reached a fire alarm and palmed it without pulling, then waited until Cassie's team flowed to a different angle and touched it with one finger. Sirens began to complain. In the confusion, he opened a door that looked locked and wasn't, because most locks just want to be asked by the right hand.

Skael and Kareth tumbled into a boiler room that had decided to be a maze. Jude took them through it like a man walking a path he'd worn into the earth years ago: left at the bleeding valve, right at the green-painted pipe with the scuffed section where a contractor's ladder had bitten a winter ago, straight through the storage cage that had lost a hinge in a renovation and kept the lie of solidity anyway.

He took a cleaning trolley by the handle and tipped it artfully, bleach spidering across the tiles. "Dogs," he said.

"We haven't seen any," Skael said.

"You won't," Jude said. "But they'll think about them. Thinking costs time."

They hit another service door, and Jude didn't try the handle because the scratched paint around the box told him the latch was sticky when it rained, and it had rained. He put his palm to the metal and shoved hard at the point where the frame had a millimeter more give than the rest. The door sighed and opened.

Outside, the alley smelled like yesterday's bread and today's cigarettes. A delivery truck idled. The driver stared at his phone with the private intimacy of a man having a better conversation than he could have with the world. Jude guided them behind the truck, counted to five so a camera's slow sweep wouldn't catch their silhouettes, then slipped them into the stream of commuters rising from the metro like steam.

He didn't tell Kareth to change his posture. He changed his own, and the others mirrored without knowing they had. The art of vanishing isn't invisibility. It's convincing the scene not to elevate you above the background.

Three men became three shapes, then became three ideas nobody in Paris needed to name.

Cassie came down the back stairs in three flights and quickly turned into the alley. She caught the tail of the siren from the fire alarm and discarded it as a story someone else would tell later. Her eyes cut the space into lanes. A delivery truck. A stack of crates. The black rectangle of a service door deciding whether to keep secrets.

She moved, weapon low, shoulders soft, like someone who knew how to run and not alarm a city by doing it. The camera on the van caught a smear of motion at the mouth of the alley. She registered three figures turning into the pedestrian flow. One tall, one broader at the shoulders, one lean in a way that read as *contained* rather than *thin.*

She raised the gun. A tourist stepped into her line, looking the wrong way. She shifted. A cyclist cut across behind the tourists like a blade. She took two steps, reopened the angle, and there was only the crowd.

"Contact?" Marsten in her ear.

She swallowed once. "Negative. Three silhouettes into the flow. No confirmation."

"You want to lock down the block?"

She scanned the faces. None were the right kind of wrong. The van's operator murmured that the seven-device cluster had fragmented into zeros and ones, and the noise was back to being noise.

"Negative," she said. "We've got what we came for."

She walked back toward the building, forcing her breath to slow. You can lose a thing you didn't have. You can also know it was there by the way the air remembers it after it's gone.

The scarred woman sat cuffed in the back of the van, her wrists ringed in plastic that had been engineered not to hurt until it did. She watched Cassie without blinking; when she did blink, it was slow, reptile-careful, as if closing her eyes were a negotiation with herself.

Cassie climbed in and crouched. She preferred to be at eye level when she could. It saved time later.

"You speak English," she said. "Or French."

The woman's mouth twitched. "You'll have my name, agent. You will have the wrong one first. Then the right one. You will look at them and not know which mattered."

"Let's start with the wrong one, then," Cassie said.

Silence. The woman was testing for the move behind the words, the way players at a board test for whether the table is level.

"You killed six of mine," the woman said at last, not angry. "You think I am going to give you the seventh without making you work for it?"

"Six of yours shot at my people and died," Cassie said. "You're the seventh because you chose not to. That choice is how you live to have another one."

The woman's eyes flickered, almost amusement. "In your Syria, did choices look like this?"

Cassie didn't let the surprise show. "Sometimes they looked like worse."

The woman said a name that was not her name. Cassie wrote it anyway. You keep the wrong names; they tell you who someone wanted to be while they were lying.

"Why France?" Cassie asked. "Why this district? Why this time?"

The woman stared at the van's roof for a moment as if reading an answer written there. "Because a plan made by people who worship old maps told us a city is a city. They are not. They are people. And people do not like to be bent."

"That's not an answer."

"It is the beginning of one," the woman said. "And beginnings are more valuable than you think."

Cassie looked at her for a long breath and closed the van door. Outside, Paris negotiated with itself as it always did. The DGSI liaison arrived late and full of the kind of courtesy that sounds like a bill. Cassie spoke to him in the same way she spoke to her mirror; briefly, without the expectation of being surprised.

In her hotel later, she wrote the report in lines the system liked to read: *Six hostile actors neutralized. One captured. No friendly losses. Communications collected. Leads developing.* When she finished, she stared at the space between *leads* and *developing* and wrote Paris pod compromised because the larger sentence would be for another day.

She stood by the window. The lights lit up the river as a trail. She let it become trajectories again until she saw three men turn into a crowd and vanish in a place where the crowd should have been just a crowd.

Kareth paced a rented room that smelled of cleaning fluid and the ghosts of other men's arguments. He wanted to convene judgment for the dead in Paris as if calling a court for people without breath would teach the living to obey. Skael told him, finally, to sit down.

"You nearly died," Skael said. "You'll learn more from that than from speech."

Kareth's eyes flared. He sat anyway.

Rakkar sent Jude the telemetry he'd stolen from the edge of Cassie's net: the comm fingerprints the pod had used when fear made them forget to bury their style; the way their glyph cadence staggered on the third byte when stress rose; the little tells that turn into keys if you collect enough of them.

"Useful," Jude said.

Rakkar nodded. "She's good," he added after a beat.

"She is," Jude agreed.

He didn't say Cassie's name. Names were a form of intimacy, and he liked to ration those. In the expanse, Vael folded his arms and regarded him through the cage with the kind of attention that feels like heat without warmth.

"You let humans cut our cousins down," Vael said.

"I let the map sharpen itself," Jude replied.

"You think knife-making is a neutral act."

"I think it is an inevitable one," Jude said. *"The knife exists. Who holds it next is the only interesting question."*

"And when the blade cuts your hand?"

Jude thought of the fact that Cassie had almost seen them. He thought of Kareth's breath turning ragged as plaster dust in his lungs. He thought of the scarred woman whispering names that would be both useful and deceitful in equal measure.

"Then I'll change how I hold it," he said.

Vael stepped closer to the bars. *"Victories become debts. Debts become chains. Even for men who believe they cannot be bound."*

Jude smiled. *"Then I'll learn to pick locks,"* he said again, and felt the cage hum once in answer like a faraway engine.

Two nights later, the same satellite hiccupped its maintenance beat, and Rakkar was there to listen. The handshake he caught this time was smaller, craftier, the kind of touch a person uses when they know someone's watching and aren't ready to stop being watched yet. It bloomed, faint, a country away.

Rakkar lifted his head. "They talk among themselves when they're afraid."

"Of us?" Jude asked lightly.

"Of everything," Rakkar said. "Us included."

Jude touched the map with one finger and felt the geometry rotate around that pressure. Pattern becomes plan. Plan becomes motion. Motion becomes story. He was good at stories. He had learned to be better at endings.

"We go again," he said.

Rakkar glanced at him sideways. "Do we acknowledge the part where Cassie Reeve is now hunting a shape that has begun to look like us?"

Jude considered this without moving anything as visible as a muscle. "She hunts what she can see. We will give her just enough of that to keep her away from what she can't."

"And if she gets closer?"

Jude thought of a quiet man holding nothing, and the way Cassie's eyes had taken the measure of absence as if it were a presence. He admired that. He registered it as a variable.

"Then we adjust," he said. "That is all any of us ever do."

He closed his eyes for a moment, and the white expanse returned, the cage glowing faintly like bone in winter light. Vael watched him without speaking, which was sometimes his most articulate form of speech.

Outside, Paris negotiated the price of breakfast. Somewhere, a woman with a scar on the bridge of her nose began to decide which truths were expensive enough to sell slow.

And across a quiet room in London, Jude Black began to shape the next day as if he had written it already and was simply reading ahead.

Chapter 12: MANHATTAN VEIL

Twelve months since the Hampshire incident

Nireva had once believed in the High Circle. Belief was what kept a soldier's hand steady when the void outside the canopy wanted to make it shake. The Circle gave orders, and orders gave meaning. For years, she'd told herself that was enough.

But time changed conviction. Even before she left, whispers had reached her: the Circle was more interested in ritual than victory, and in ceremony than survival. She had worn the uniform anyway, commanded units that bled anyway. The habit of loyalty outlives the reason for it.

Landing here had confirmed her doubts. Earth was raw, unshaped, and yet the Circle had sent them to seed it with nothing but fragments from stolen archives four decades out of date. Improvised targets. Outdated maps. A plan that sounded like hope pretending to be a strategy. She might have called it sabotage by neglect if she hadn't known better.

So she had done what soldiers do when doctrine fails: made her own plan. The pod embedded in Washington as staffers, aides, researchers, voices in committees no one watched. She herself became Jennifer Graves, congresswoman, a mask she wore as easily as breathing. For a year, they pushed quietly, testing where the system bent, cataloguing who listened too eagerly, who drank too much, or who believed in the myths their own party whispered to itself.

Then came the message. A signal shaped wrong, too careful to be an accident. The UK pod reaching across the Atlantic.

She had not expected them, after all this time. Nor had she expected the names inside it: Kareth, loud, predictable. And Vael.

That was the part that unsettled her. Not the message, not even the risk. The names. If it was true, then the Circle had miscalculated again, and if it was false, then someone was playing at a game only Vael had the patience to teach.

Either way, when they arrived in New York, she would find out what it was they wanted. And why now?

The Hudson glimmered dull steel under a low sky as the four of them disembarked. New York in autumn was a noise that never stopped; sirens, horns, the crush of a city convinced the world spun around it.

Tom-Zherin craned his neck upward at the skyline, grinning in spite of himself. "Bloody hell. Every film I've ever watched, and it still looks taller in person."

Jude gave him the faintest smile. "Careful. Staring up is how they spot tourists."

Kareth walked ahead without looking, shoulders taut, every motion purposeful. Skael hung back, scanning doorways and rooftops like a bodyguard too tired to pretend he wasn't.

Tom-Zherin leaned closer to Jude as they hailed a cab. "He always like this?

Jude smirked. "Kareth believes every step he takes is history. Don't interrupt him."

The cab ride uptown was filled with Tom-Zherin's commentary—Yankees caps, steam rising from grates, and the sheer impossibility of Times Square. Jude let him talk. Sometimes listening was easier than silencing. And it felt as if more of the real Tom was coming out.

The lift climbed like judgment.

Kareth watched his reflection shiver in the brushed steel and forced his jaw to unclench. Paris had been a room full of small people, smaller air, powder and plaster dust, and voices that thought they were louder than fate. He could still feel the ache in his throat from the gas, the weight of Skael's hand on his collar, dragging him half-blind through a corridor that refused to open. Worst of all, the other voice—calm and surgical in his ear, guiding him left, then down, then through. Vael's voice. Not a commander's bark or a zealot's chant. A scalpel. The humiliation of being saved had lodged in Kareth like grit. It made every swallow taste of iron.

He replayed the moment again: the door that wouldn't yield; the chain biting; the panic yawning; then Vael, in his host body, stepping out of shadow as if he'd always been there, as if he'd *meant* to arrive at the precise second Kareth needed him. It had felt like a rescue. It felt, now, like choreography.

The lift opened on glass and skyline. He straightened his coat and stepped into the apartment of a woman who looked at cities the way mathematicians look at proofs; already solved, merely waiting to be written down. Jennifer Graves, the congresswoman, to the cameras. Nireva to those who mattered.

He would win her. He would correct the map.

The apartment was glass and steel above Central Park, a political donor's dream. Nireva wore the mask well, power-dresser, early forties, dark hair in a sculpted wave, every movement deliberate.

"Gentlemen," she said, and the word cut the air like a gavel. "Welcome to New York."

Kareth bowed slightly, formal, rehearsed. Skael nodded once, silent. Tom-Zherin, awkward in his jacket, tried for charm. "Lovely place you've got."

Her eyes lingered on him a beat longer than necessary, cataloguing. Then they moved to Jude. She smiled, thin, assessing. "And you are?"

"An associate," Jude said easily. "We've come a long way."

"Some farther than others," Nireva said, before turning her back to pour drinks.

They sat in a lounge framed by glass. Central Park spread beneath like a rug. Nireva asked questions the way surgeons cut—precise, with no wasted motion.

"What have you accomplished in London?" she asked.

"Survival," Jude said.

"Discipline," Kareth countered.

"Patience," Skael added.

Tom-Zherin hesitated. "Adjustment."

Nireva's eyebrow arched. "Adjustment?"

Tom-Zherin flushed. "We... we're not exactly where we thought we'd be. But we're here, aren't we?"

For the first time, her smile seemed genuine. "Honesty. Rare in this company."

Kareth stiffened. Jude leaned back, hiding his amusement.

Kareth and Nireva entered into a separate room, just the two of them. Vael had given the instruction for Kareth to lead this UK delegation, with him observing and not revealing himself.

She poured him whiskey with the economical grace of someone for whom hospitality was just another instrument. "No Vael?" she asked, feeling suspicious; she had the kind of eyes that scanned to find anything out of the ordinary.

"Kings confer alone," Kareth said and smiled, taking the glass. He chose the window rather than the chair, framed himself against Central Park as though the city were a cloak he had chosen to wear.

"Are you a king?" Nireva asked mildly.

"I am what follows a soft generation," he said. "And softness is everything I see when I look at this world. They parade their institutions like armor. They are paper. You press. They tear."

"And yet you tore first," she said, not looking up from the bottle. "Paris."

He let the heat rise and then forced it down. "A misreading," he said, almost convincing himself. "An overabundance of caution from a cell that mistook hiding for cunning. It is corrected."

"Corrected how?" A tilt of her head. A scalpel sliding under skin.

"Survival of the fittest." He set his glass down, as if the movement were an order and the table would obey. "You know what must be done. This... seeding, this patient rot-the-beams, it wastes advantage. We should push. Replace key hands. Make the doors open before the fleet arrives, not after. Move committees, ministries, command posts. I can move them."

"And who will you be replacing?" She moved closer, the city behind her like circuitry. "Who bends? Who breaks? Speak plainly."

"Congress," he said, tasting the word she wore like a coat. "Agencies. Allies. The old Atlantic links. Your links. They are brittle. With your cover as it is, you can place levers. I can pull them."

She didn't smile. Not quite. "And whose levers would you pull on command, Kareth? The High Circle's?"

He allowed himself a brief, disdainful laugh. "The Circle is a council of children clinging to old maps. They wait at wormhole checkpoints as if the Assembly will forget how to count. They sent us to seed. Fine. We seeded. The ground is ready."

She watched him the way a hawk watches a field.

He felt the urge to sweeten the air with certainty. To make the room smaller and his voice larger. "I do not speak as a supplicant," he said. "I speak with the authority you remember. Vael's authority."

The name changed the temperature. He saw the flicker behind her eyes, not an expression so much as a memory arriving. The pause had weight.

"Vael," she said, the syllable careful as a key. "You invoke him easily."

"We travel with him," Kareth said, because the room felt like a test and he would not be found wanting. "He is with us now. Cautious," he added, because he could not leave it there, because the humiliation in Paris still scraped. "Too cautious. He lets... other considerations slow his hand. I would not."

Silence. The city breathed against the glass.

Nireva set her glass down without a sound. "Vael," she repeated, and this time it wasn't a question. "Here."

Kareth felt the mistake land inside him like a small, clean blade. He smiled to blunt it. "We thought it wise not to advertise."

"I want to see him." She didn't raise her voice. She didn't have to. The sentence arrived, and the room rearranged itself to fit it.

"I can speak for..."

"No." She crossed to the door and opened it with a hand that never trembled. "I asked to see Vael."

For an instant, pride reared up, ugly and bright. He wanted to say that his words were Vael's words; that the cadence in his mouth carried as much weight as any other. He swallowed it, because swallowing is also a kind of strength.

"As you wish," he said, and managed not to break the glass when he set it down.

The corridor held the kind of tasteful art people buy when they want to be seen as serious. Kareth closed the study door behind him, smoothing his face into something that did not look like defeat.

Jude was already there, leaning against the wall as if the building had been designed to give him that posture. He wasn't reading his phone. He wasn't pretending not to be waiting. He simply occupied space like a fact.

For a heartbeat, they said nothing. Then something like realization cut across Kareth's features, too quick to be a flinch, too honest to be anything else. He saw it: the way Vael had insisted he go in first; the way the evening had been paced; the way Paris had been allowed to happen in the exact shape required to make this moment inevitable. The trap had not felt like a trap until it closed.

Jude's expression did not change. If there was a smile, it was microscopic, flickering in the muscles at the corner of his mouth.

"She asked for Vael," Kareth said, and hated the way the word tasted when he had to hand it over.

"Then we should not keep her waiting," Jude said gently.

Kareth stepped aside. He made room for Vael to take the plaudits for the second time in a week and said nothing while his pride bled.

The study felt smaller with the door closed, as if the city had stepped back to let something older take the room. Nireva stood by the bookshelves, one hand on a spine as though she might steady herself on language.

Jude entered without ceremony. He didn't hurry. He didn't slow. He crossed the space with the unarguable cadence of a commander who had never once doubted the rightness of arrival.

"Jennifer," he said, and put just enough of Vael's weight into the name to make it mean something it wasn't. Not Jennifer. Nireva.

Her head lifted as if a string had been pulled. The careful mask cracked for a moment, and the person under it looked out. "Vael," she breathed.

In the expanse, Vael struck the bars so hard Jude felt the ripple in his teeth. "*Do not...*"

"*Be quiet,*" Jude told him, without moving his lips. He let the echo of Vael's own command tone shape the word. The cage thrummed.

He took one step closer, then another, erasing the space until the air had to choose which of them to carry. He didn't touch her. Touch would come later, when he chose it. For now, the intimacy was at a distance.

"You have been busy," he said, and the syllables weren't just sound, they were memory—Vael's cadence riding Jude's tongue, the unteachable rhythm that had carried men across black space and not broken.

"I thought you were dead," Nireva said, and in the way she said it, Jude heard all the pragmatic months built on that idea, suddenly embarrassed to be wrong.

She came to him then, not closing the last inch, stopping close enough that he could see the hairline crack in the pearl of her earring. "Say something I would know. Say something only I would hear."

Jude had prepared for this without telling himself he had prepared. He let the expanse unspool, held the cage while he took what he needed. The dunes at Kar Tal at night, black glass under three moons. The oath made at the basalt arch on Suran's Spine. The smell of metal and rain in the bunk corridor outside Deck Five, the night before the Targ raid. He chose one carefully and handed it back to her like a coin placed on a tongue.

"The basalt arch," he said softly. "Your glove tore as we climbed. You bled and wouldn't stop, and when I told you to go back, you asked me if I was in the habit of losing my way right before the summit."

Her eyes filled and did not spill. She put her fingers to her wrist, once, as if confirming a pulse. "It *is* you."

In the cage, Vael's fury reached a bright, cold peak that felt like silence turned to blade. "*Those memories are mine!*"

Jude did not flinch. He had learned to hold two truths in his mouth until one of them bent. "The Circle would have you wait," he said. "They would have you trust in patience disguised as doctrine. That is not my way. It was never ours."

"Then say the word," she whispered. She had never looked so like a human as she did in that moment, human not as weakness but as choice. "Say it, and I will move the pieces they gave me. Committee chairs. Oversight calendars. The small doors that open into larger rooms."

He let himself breathe once, slow. "We move," he said. "But we move in a way that feels like the city choosing us. No ruptures. No banners. Pressure, here." He reached for a pen from her desk and tapped the leather blotter with it, marking invisible points as he named them. "Appropriations. Staff director level, not the members; they will follow the rails they are given. A hearing widened by twelve minutes on a Thursday; nothing gets done in twelve minutes unless it was decided last week. A rider on a rider on a bill that pretends to fund nothing and quietly starves an office on K Street that coordinates allies who think they are coordinating you."

She watched his hand like some people watch storms, fear and awe in equal parts. "And Kareth?"

"Kareth is a hammer," Jude said, and allowed himself the smallest smile. "We will need him when it is time to break. Until then, he can practice being heavy in rooms where heaviness reads as sincerity."

"He believes you slow him," she said, testing, probing.

"Let him," Jude said. "He is easier to steer when he thinks he is tugging the reins."

Nireva moved the final inch, not a touch but the *idea* of one becoming real. Her fingers came to rest at his wrist, pulse to pulse, the intimacy of people who had fought back to back and believed it meant something beyond tactics.

"You are cruel," she said, and there was something like admiration in it. "You bring me back to a war I had learned to name with other words."

"I bring you back to yourself," he said, and every word was a door opening.

Her eyes closed, once. When she opened them, the decision had been made. "Then I am yours," she said quietly. "Not the Circle's. Not the boy with slogans. Yours."

In the expanse, Vael sank against the bars, as if the memory of warmth hurt his bones. "*She is mine*," he said, almost tender in the way rage can be when it remembers love.

"You will have her," Jude told him without pity, *"when you have a body."*

He felt the cage flex, then hold.

Nireva stepped away first because she understood theatre as well as war. She crossed to the window and looked down at the park, the running paths that pretended to be wild, and the lamps that confessed the lie. "I'll need names," she said. "Of staffers. Of rooms. Of doors I should leave ajar."

"You'll have them before morning," he said. "From a man who doesn't know yet that he works for you."

Her smile was small and devastating. "Welcome home, Vael."

He inclined his head, accepting the coronation he had written for himself.

When he opened the door, Kareth was still in the corridor, pretending the painting opposite interested him. Jude didn't slow. He didn't need to. Kareth's eyes flicked up as he passed, hunting for something to strike. Jude gave him nothing. The faintest nod. A private acknowledgement of an orchestration completed.

Behind him, Nireva's voice drifted from the study, cool and bright as cut glass: "Send in your associate who handles logistics. We have work."

Jude didn't look back. He rarely did. The plan was moving. The city had decided it, because he had taught it how.

Cassie had tracked them here the old-fashioned way: paper before pixels. Two passports flagged by Europol in Paris, the same names surfacing in JFK arrivals. Jude Black. Michael Ashworth.

It was late afternoon when she spotted them following a tipoff: four men crossing Central Park near Bethesda Terrace, walking with the casual rhythm of people who knew exactly where they were going. Jude was in the middle, flanked by Michael's rigid posture and Leo's silent watchfulness. Tom, the most human of them, kept talking with a smile that didn't belong in this city.

Cassie's heart clenched. She had them.

Then Jude's head tilted, just slightly. His gaze brushed over a saxophonist, a jogger, a couple walking a dog, and her. Not a pause. Not a double-take. Just the faint acknowledgment of a predator who knew when he was being observed.

A moment later, they split. Too clean to be an accident. Four lines parting across the park, each man peeling away with the grace of rehearsed geometry.

Cassie swore under her breath and chose. Jude. Always Jude.

He didn't hurry. That was the unnerving part. He walked with the kind of composure that made everyone else look frantic, blending into the city's rhythm. Cassie shadowed from thirty paces, weaving through strollers and dog-walkers.

Halfway across the Mall, she swore she saw his hand brush against a tourist's tote bag. A folded leaflet appeared between his fingers, palmed so smoothly that even she barely caught it. Ten steps later, he dropped it. A man stooped to grab it, confused, stepping directly into Cassie's path.

"Sorry," she muttered, skirting him, heart thudding. By the time she cleared the distraction, Jude was another twenty meters ahead, adjusting his cuff like nothing had happened.

At the 59th Street station, he descended into the subway. Cassie followed, catching the turnstile just before it closed. He boarded the first car; she slipped into the second, standing by the door. Through the connecting window, she saw him: posture relaxed, one hand on the rail, eyes never quite on her but aware.

The train rattled into motion. Cassie felt the stare like static, even when he looked away. It wasn't evasion. It was theater; *I know you're there, and I want you to know I know.*

At Chambers Street, he stepped off. She followed, pushing through commuters. He didn't run. He drifted into the crush, then out again, always a few steps ahead.

Tribeca narrowed around them, glass towers giving way to brick and shadows. Cassie's breathing quickened. He knew these streets; she could feel it. Every turn seemed designed to stretch the distance without breaking it, to keep her chasing without closing.

Finally, in a narrow service alley, he glanced back once. A calm, unreadable expression. Then he turned a corner.

Cassie pushed after him, weapon close to her hip. The alley emptied into another street, alive with traffic. He was gone.

She scanned furiously, doorways, stairwells, mirrors of glass. Nothing. He'd slipped her, again.

Cassie leaned against the wall, chest tight. That was twice now; Paris, and her. And each time he'd made sure she knew just enough to believe she was close.

Marsten's voice buzzed in her ear. "Got him?"

Cassie stared at the crowd, swallowing her quarry. "Negative contact," she said. "But it's him. It's always him."

Jude found Tom-Zherin in a diner on Lexington. Neon buzzed against greasy glass. Tom pushed a plate of fries around, uneaten.

"You alright?" Jude asked.

Tom-Zherin shrugged. "Dunno. Feels like I've stepped off a curb and I'm waiting to hit the ground. Good thing Nate-Rakkar flagged CIA chatter before we came."

"I keep thinking back to us... the human 'us'. Uni. Those nights in London, when you'd somehow get us past every bouncer, talk our way into clubs we had no business being in."

Jude smiled faintly. "Your host, Tom, always carried the conversation. I just nudged the right doors."

Tom-Zherin chuckled. "Nah. You bent things. You always did. Made them go your way. Saved my arse more times than I care to count. Remember Brighton? That copper nearly had me."

Jude remembered. He'd talked fast, pulled strings, turned suspicion into trust. Even then.

Tom-Zherin's voice softened. "Just... don't let it bend you out of shape, mate. The world needs at least one of us to stay sane."

Jude looked at him. For a moment, he almost wished Tom-Zherin hadn't said it. That kind of trust was heavy. Dangerous.

In the expanse, Vael's voice stirred. "*This one is too human. He will betray you, not by choice, but by weakness. Either that, or Zherin is in control and testing you.*"

Jude didn't answer. He finished his coffee and smiled at Tom-Zherin as though the weight wasn't there.

In her penthouse, Nireva stared out at Manhattan's lights. Vael intrigued her. Kareth bored her. She would choose carefully, but she was already leaning toward the one who carried silence like a weapon.

On a rooftop, Cassie lit a cigarette she wouldn't finish. She replayed the chase in her head, convinced the ghost she'd seen was the same shadow from Paris. "*Next time,*" she told herself. "*Next time I'll have him.*"

And from his hotel room, Jude stood once more in the expanse. Vael's outline leaned against the cage. "*She is a mirror,*" he said of Nireva. "*Look too long, and you will see yourself as prey.*"

Jude smiled faintly. "*Then I'll make sure the reflection is mine to control.*"

He was cognizant of the fact he had put Nireva and her US pod 'in play'. But it was a calculated move to ensure they moved the way he wanted them to, as slow or fast as needed. To either make them slip and get caught, or help in his wider plan to save humanity from the impending Aethero invasion; a plan he was having to formulate without seeing all of the chess pieces.

The cage pulsed once, like the city's heartbeat.

Chapter 13:
DIVERGENCE

Fourteen months since the Hampshire incident

The jet cut east through a slate morning, white contrails sewing a line from London to a city of glass. On the leather seats, Tom-Zherin tried to sleep and couldn't. His host's uncle's tail number bought them the kind of discretion you can't rent on a commercial flight; handlers at both ends would call it 'facilitation', which was a polite word for the world bending if you knew where to press.

"Feels wrong, using family like this," Tom-Zherin said, low enough that only Jude heard.

"Feels efficient," Jude replied, not unkind. "We need clean ingress. This gives us two borders and one story."

Kareth sat forward, elbows on knees, watching clouds with the intensity of a man bullying weather into compliance. Skael stared at an iPad that wasn't on. Somewhere over Siberia, the cabin fell into the heavy silence of men saving their strength for the landing.

They came down at Hongqiao because private jets are less interesting there. The FBO lounge smelled of tea and lemon polish; a woman in a navy jacket stamped things without ever appearing to look at them. Past the tinted glass, the high-speed rail concourse unfurled like a cathedral to motion—fifteen platforms under a ribbed roof, trains in long white livery arriving to the minute.

Shanghai greeted them with a sleek kind of certainty. QR codes blinked on every surface; cameras watched without blinking. The city had taught itself to move millions like water in a lock, sluicing forward in obedient pulses. Jude admired it the way a safecracker admires a vault: not for its virtue, but for the quality of the problem it presented.

Tom-Zherin's host had been here thrice before and had learned to read the city's manners. "Points for everything," he said, half to himself, as they watched a group of commuters scan into a bike-rack. "Pay on your phone, rent your life on your phone, rate your neighbor on your phone if he parks wrong. The *soft* fences are the strong ones."

"Soft fences keep herds tame," Kareth said.

"Until someone paints a new gate in the same color," Jude murmured.

They took the inner ring road into Pudong, past towers that looked like ideas someone had been brave enough to make permanent. The driver said little. Jude said less.

The local pod met them in a private room high above the river. Pudong spread beneath them like an architect's rendering, glass that hadn't yet learned fatigue. The room was quiet in an expensive way, the HVAC tuned to be felt but not heard.

They rose as one when Jude entered. Seven hosts, like the Paris cell had been, but where Paris had been rough-edged and jumpy, this group moved with the efficiency of a courtiers' school. The woman at their center wore a charcoal suit and an expression that said she knew precisely which poems to quote at which dinners. She inclined her head, respectful, not deferential.

"Takra Vael," she said, using the old honorific as if she were laying down a piece on a board. "Welcome. I am Seyra, but here they call me Lin Qiao."

Kareth straightened at the title, hungry for reflected light. Jude gave the woman the faintest nod. "Report."

She did not ask for pleasantries. "We have embedded at three levels," she said. "Party School, where the next five years are told in whispers before they are written. Cadres at provincial finance, small levers with long arms. And logistics at Waigaoqiao and Yangshan.

"Waigaoqiao for noise, too much movement for anyone to pin down. Yangshan for leverage, cleaner lanes, and predictable schedules. Boxes enter the bloodstream through both."

Another man, a slight figure with a technician's hands, added, "Ministry of State Security, mid-tier. Not glamorous. Useful. We know which meetings matter because we control the calendars."

"The army?" Skael asked.

"District-level PLA," the woman said. "We don't touch the Central Military Commission. That would be a confession. But brigades take their signals from places we can bend."

Kareth's mouth curved. "You have done in months what others pretend to do in years."

"Our landscape makes it easier," the woman said. "The system likes an efficient story. We learned to write ours in its grammar."

Tom-Zherin stood by the window, looking down at the gray ribbon of the Huangpu, where barges shouldered past tourist boats imitating old wooden shapes. "What happens when the system asks what your story costs?"

Qiao glanced at him, filing the question under *human noise,* then back to Jude. "Your guidance, Takra."

Jude stepped to the table. They had laid out a map, not of the city but of decision, lines connecting acronyms to names to rooms to times of day. It was the kind of lattice you build when you believe yourself invulnerable because you can see far. He admired the craftsmanship. He distrusted the arrogance.

"You've done well," he said, and meant it. "You've chosen levers that don't scream when pulled."

"We don't scream," Kareth said, pleased to be in the chorus.

Jude set his palm on the map, marking four points without touching them. "Keep your hands off central propaganda. It looks like power; it is spotlight. Keep your hands *on* logistics; it is shadow. If you need to move men, move paper first. It's quieter."

Qiao nodded once, approving. "We came to the same conclusions."

"Good," Jude said. "Then you will come to this one: you are strong enough to be noticed by your cousins."

A flicker passed among them, the slightest tightening under the eyes. The fear not of enemies, but of allies.

"We've seen traces," the slight man said. "Old syntax on a new line."

"France is gone," Kareth said, making it a trophy. "The survivors speak badly when they speak at all."

"And you shouldn't count corpses as proof of your wisdom," Jude said mildly.

Silence stretched, then smoothed. Qiao smiled as if at a good move on a chessboard. "We are not children, Takra. We bow to you. We do not bow to panic."

Jude smiled back, all teeth hidden. "See that you don't."

In the expanse, Vael murmured, approval in the shape of caution. *"They are competent. They are also proud. Pride breaks at the wrong angle."*

"Then we will choose the angle," Jude thought.

They slept at a hotel with carpets that drank sound. Tom-Zherin knocked on Jude's door around midnight with two beers and the look of a man who needed to be nearer to the person he trusted because the floor kept tilting.

"Do you ever feel it?" he asked, leaning on the balcony rail, watching the reflections of light stack themselves wrong in the river's small chop. "Like the world's a stage someone keeps rotating under your feet, and all you can do to pretend you're not dizzy is talk like you meant it?"

"Sometimes," Jude said.

Tom-Zherin smiled at that, grateful for the unvarnished honesty that came once every twenty reassurances. "Private jet. Women and men in suits who think they own the future. You telling everyone where to stand. And still..." He moved his hand as if feeling for a seam in the air. "Still feels like someone else is pulling the strings."

"Who do you think that would be?" Jude asked.

Tom-Zherin considered. "Whatever we became in Hampshire. Or whoever we let in."

Jude didn't answer, it was too painful to see what was previously his friend act this way. He watched a freight stack slip past under a bridge and thought about boxes with the wrong labels and the right contents.

Before Tom-Zherin left, he hesitated. "If I started... feeling things. Like him. Like *me* before him. You'd tell me, right? Before it got... bad."

Jude let a beat pass. "I would."

Tom-Zherin heard the lie and forgave it because that's what friendship is when you need it enough.

Cassie Reeve didn't call it an obsession when she justified the late-night spreadsheet to herself. She called it pattern recognition. Patterns don't lie; people do.

Europol's Paris flag had given her two names she could carry through from one airport to another, Jude Black and Michael Ashworth. Global entry logs, FBO schedules. The fingerprints of men who thought they were invisible and had simply learned to blur differently.

"China," she said with David in her office, because naming is how you prove you're not guessing.

"China," Marsten agreed on the phone, sounding as tired as the line. "And before you ask, we're not green-lit for unilateral ops."

"They're not unilateral," David said. "The targets are multinational. We're following a network. You know the brief."

"I also know the Paris prisoner was judged unreliable," Marsten said. "And that half the men we shot had CVs that say 'respectable' and phone histories that say 'very not respectable,' which makes everyone up the chain want to treat it like a right-wing fever dream that happened to acquire funding and access. It fits a box they already have."

"It fits a box because they're lazy," Cassie snapped. "You saw what she said."

"I saw what she screamed," Marsten corrected. "About race superiority and cleansing and birthright. That rhetoric is older than your grandparents. It makes it easy to file and forget."

"Russia?" Cassie said. "If this were a state thing, Moscow would be tidal in the noise right now. It isn't. They just rolled up a similar cell and took credit."

"Which also fits the box," Marsten said. "But I hear you. What do you want?"

"Liaison in Shanghai," she said. "Not an army. One car. Two ears. Room to breathe."

"I can give you a consulate desk and a driver who doesn't get lost," he said. "You'll get two ears if you rent the second. And I'll come too."

"That'll do," Cassie said, and meant "I'll do more with it than they expect."

When she hung up, she stared at the line on her screen that had swung from JFK to PVG with surgical neatness. Jude Black. Michael Ashworth. And two of the others.

In Whitehall, Ella sat with a cup of tea that had gone cold during the act of believing it would stay warm if she looked at it enough. The MoD database glowed with its usual charity, the kind that gives you enough to think you understand and not enough to be right. She had permission to see what the civil servants called "cross-cutting anomalies," which was another way of saying *things that get in the way of other things you wanted to do.*

The names weren't supposed to reappear. That was the point of leaving Hampshire behind: you get to bury the night, and the events stay buried with it. And yet here they were, one by one, attached to files that had no reason to touch hers. Jude, flagged in a briefing about financial flows with too many verbs and insufficient subjects. Tom, surfacing in a line about "liaison with private aviation operators." And together with Mike and Leo, brushing a customs entry that had been redacted into politeness.

Adeel's name appeared like a stain in the margins. He had always been good at feeding useful things. Lately, the useful has shifted to the interesting, which is the kind of useful that kills people.

Ella closed her laptop gently and sat quiet, letting it feel like a decision rather than a failure to make one. She thought to herself, *"there are moments when agency is only agency if you use it badly."*

She booked a flight ticket to Shanghai.

The Chinese pod favored a teahouse for their informal briefings, walls of dark wood, a long counter where a man with beautiful hands poured water that thought it was being judged. Qiao had told Jude the place was "safe," which is a claim you should never believe, but sometimes you let other people be comforted by their illusions so they stay close to you while they're making them.

That night, the table was covered with state money arranged not to look like state money. The printouts ran like irrigation ditches across parched land: appropriations columns; vendor IDs; shipping lanes; quarterly deliverables. There was a pleasure to that order, Qiao admitted privately. Battle had its own elegance; so did budgets.

"They read as flu," she said, tapping a table where someone in the Ministry of Health had signed a two-page memo with a sentence long enough to hide an elephant. "Seasonal spikes, rural clinics, three states that always cry wolf this time of year. No one is asking why a lab in Zhangjiang is producing synthetic protein to be shipped by a contractor who usually handles veterinary supplies."

Kareth picked the paper up and read the line twice. "And in truth?"

"Adaptation." She didn't soften the word. "If the body is a system and the environment is hostile, you intervene. You make the air less sharp. You make the food less poisonous. You teach the immune code a new song. Necessary, because this planet is protected, not covered by the Assembly influence-sphere vaccine we copied and cultivated for our own kind."

Kareth smiled in a way that mistook the room for a parade ground. "So when our soldiers arrive, they will not drown in their air."

"They will breathe," she agreed. "They will not die of what you call a cold. They will not infect and fall. Logistics will still kill men faster than bullets. We are at least moving one kind of logistics out of the casualty column. To the Assembly, this world is a nature reserve. A preserve for primitives. Untouched, unvisited, unvaccinated. To us, that makes it open ground."

Jude didn't sit. He rarely did. He had drifted to the end of the table where the line items thickened. "Split the contracts," he said. "By amount and agency. Scatter the signatures. It looks like five people making small decisions, not one program begging to be noticed."

"Good," she replied. "And we have staff, assistant staff, on the calendar flow. Appropriations is a river. We put stones in it. The stream moves around them and forgets it meant to run straight. Budgets look accidental when we design them that way."

Jude scanned the shape of the room like a man who could feel where it would break.

"Timelines," he said, and she heard what he didn't put into the plural: how long until a body that has been born elsewhere can breathe long enough here to lead?

"Three months for the bulk," she said. "Less if no one asks questions. More if someone notices the shape of the boxes."

He looked up long enough for their eyes to catch. The look was not approval. It was an accountant's nod: numbers added, a sum accepted. She paused and tried a small assurance. "We have fifty samples ready for the first small group that arrives."

Qiao knew why it made her chest hurt. Memory was inconvenient at this distance. She broke eye contact first and reached for another file.

She didn't know that Jude was immediately thinking of ways to bend or blunt the cultivation process.

"We want to open a corridor through the port," the slight man had said. Jude had learnt earlier that his human name was Chen Wei. "Nothing flashy. One container stream in three. The customs inspector rotates out in six weeks. We already have the replacement. It will look like diligence."

"Corridors work both ways," Jude said. "Make one and you must be ready for someone to walk back through it wearing your shoes."

Qiao poured tea without spilling. "We will burn the corridor when it has taught us what we need to know."

"What you need to know," Jude said, "is that corridors attract attention you can't see. Make your run, then close the door and open a different one three blocks away, next month, in a building with the same number of steps up and one fewer down."

"You speak like a man who has built mazes," she said.

"I prefer to walk out of them," Jude said.

Tom-Zherin watched the ceremony outside and thought about pattern, control, and how small rituals made large ones easier to accept. He caught himself smiling at a boy who leaned in past his mother to watch the steam. The boy smiled back because boys do. Tom-Zherin's chest hurt suddenly, in the quiet way that said *you remember who you were.*

Kareth noticed and filed it under *weakness.*

They rented a workspace near the docks, glass meeting rooms around a concrete core, the kind of aspirational space you lease by the month when you want to pretend an idea is already a company. The windows looked toward Waigaoqiao's cranes. The excuse was proximity. The reality was confidence. From there, Jude built the skeleton of a trap.

He stared at the lab run-sheet Qiao had left visible for too long and decided which part of it had to catch fire first.

He had left a trail before, but this path would be spelled out for someone who could read in reverse. He angled a cipher thread, corrupted but not too cleverly, through a satellite buoy that the CIA's network habitually flirted with in international waters. He bought three burner phones in three different districts and let one cross two cell towers in a pattern that would look like a man changing his mind at the last second. He paid cash for a week's worth of coffee with a card that would appear to come from the private equity fund that had bought Tom's uncle's second-favorite hobby into solvency.

He let the camera at a minor gate catch him at the exact angle he preferred to be seen, profile turned, stride uninterested. He walked like someone to be overlooked, which is how you become someone who is noticed by the person you want to notice you.

"Breadcrumbs," Vael said, watching him set the table with nothing that looked like knives.

"Directions," Jude said. *"For a particular reader."*

"Cassie Reeve."

Jude didn't confirm. He didn't need to.

At night, in the expanse, Vael pressed his palms to the bars in the way that means *this is the part where you pretend necessity is virtue. "You risk my own to sharpen an enemy again."*

"I prune," Jude said.

"You hide indulgence behind metaphor."

"I choose which fires to let burn," Jude said. *"This pod is dry wood. It will blaze. The right eyes will see the light."*

"And Ella?" Vael asked suddenly, not because the question belonged there but because he meant it to hurt, a threat.

Jude let that pass without answering, which is another kind of admission.

Cassie arrived on a wet afternoon, turning the city's neon into watercolor. The consulate driver was a careful man who pretended not to speak Mandarin when it would be inconvenient to have understood what had been said. She let him drop her a block shy of the hotel and walked the last hundred meters so the room could learn she wasn't a car.

Her Shanghai liaison was competent and underpowered. She drank her coffee black in a way that broadcast resourcefulness and lack of sleep. "We don't get to play cowboys," the woman said with a shrug that wasn't really a shrug. "We offer information. People higher than us decide things with it."

"I've met people like that," Cassie said.

They built a net as wide as two people can build without tripping alarms: cameras that didn't belong to them but would look without asking why; a municipal contractor with loose morals and a tighter mortgage who sold them a day's worth of backdoor access to a small slice of the port feeds; a Stingray that sat inside a van that looked like a van that had been parked on that street every night for a year. Cassie walked the Bund with a hat low enough to read as *don't look at me* and a posture that said *I belong here*.

The first breadcrumb arrived two days later, wrapped in ordinary ugliness: a badly formatted email to a vendor whose invoices didn't go to that address; a line that referenced a container number that had never belonged to that shipment; a timestamp that made sense only if you had been watching the last ten that hadn't. Cassie smiled without softness. Sometimes the universe brings you stories. Sometimes the storyteller is a man who wants you at a particular page at a particular time.

She went anyway. Because you can learn the habits of a storyteller by letting him think he's telling it well.

Ella's plane crossed at night and arrived in the glare. She spent thirty-two minutes at passport control rehearsing two versions of why she was here and decided not to use either of them. The city hit her the way it hits everyone who was expecting a memory of China and found a real place instead. It moved. It glittered. It watched itself in a glass.

She texted no one. She had learned that lesson long before Hampshire and had not forgotten it when it might have saved her something she didn't know she'd lost.

In a taxi, she watched a woman in the next lane peel an orange and feed slices to a child without looking down. The child's mouth accepted them on faith. Ella thought about faith, what it cost to keep it, and whether Jude still deserved any of hers.

Her hotel room smelled like the idea of clean. She put her bag down, opened the curtains, and waited for the city to explain itself to her. When it didn't, she did the thing she had promised herself she wouldn't. She typed Jude's name into a message window and didn't press send. Then she closed the window and waited in a different way.

On the fourth day, the Chinese pod brought Jude a plan dressed as a gift. By then, the first "environmental assay" orders had cleared the Waigaoqiao ledger; Yangshan's lanes were booked for the next cycle.

"A demonstration," the woman said. "We move a set of goods from a bonded Waigaoqiao warehouse under the noses of men who think they are awake. We show you our craft."

"And you show me your exposure," Jude said. "Very well."

He placed two calls on two burner phones and let one of them be overheard by a person who had been paid three thousand yuan not to ask whom she had heard speaking. He sent a third message through a glyph that would ping a machine in a Langley-adjacent basement. He set the rendezvous time for a point in the evening when the port would be wet, the light would be wrong for cameras, and the human eye would betray itself twice a minute.

That night, he stood with the local Aethero contingent on a mezzanine above a warehouse floor where laborers moved boxes with the efficiency of ants and the carelessness of men who have done this motion so many times their bodies dream it. He stood slightly behind Qiao and ahead of Kareth, which is how you stand when you intend to own the credit if it goes well and not the blame if it doesn't.

Below, a forklift turned, a pallet slid, and someone cursed softly in Shanghainese. The Qiao leaned toward Jude. "We have arranged for the inspector to be late."

"And for the replacement to be early," Jude said, not a question.

She smiled. "You do know how to read."

"Better than most," Jude said.

Far across the yard, a van that always parked there didn't. Three other vans that never parked there did. The headlights held too long and then died. Jude's pulse didn't change. In a building to the left, a dark window that had always been dark woke and became a rectangle of observation.

Kareth picked up the shift before Tom-Zherin did. Tom-Zherin picked it up because Kareth moved, the way you look where someone else is looking without knowing why. Skael didn't move at all. He had learned that movement is a choice you only get to make once per problem.

The woman's hand tightened on the rail. "Who?"

"Everyone," Jude said calmly. "Don't blink."

He pictured the Pudong lab's stainless runs going dark and decided Qiao's map was too competent to survive.

But he had built this moment for later, not tonight. The plan was supposed to ripen slowly, the noose tightening in silence until every player stepped into it by choice. Instead, the air cracked early, the teeth of the trap already closing.

Cassie's team was too small to mount anything more than a watch and a call. The PLA detail would arrive when it suited them, not when it mattered. The pod would be brave first and clever later, which is the wrong order for living long.

Jude put a hand on Tom-Zherin's arm, unthinking, and felt the flinch; the quick, shocked recognition of human touch as comfort. Tom-Zherin looked at him, and in that glance, Jude saw the entire cost of every decision he was making articulated without sound.

He took his hand away. "Time to go," he said.

"Go where?" Kareth asked, angry at the shape of the night for not matching the shape of his speech.

"Forward," Jude said calmly, already moving. "Before the fire chooses for us."

They ghosted down a stairwell that smelled of oil and rain. Behind them, the warehouse floor began to wake in the wrong way. Someone blew a whistle that meant nothing. Someone else shouted in Mandarin in a tone that meant everything. Cassie was out there somewhere, listening to the city countdown.

Jude smiled, small and private. The divergence had begun. The pieces would fall; he would decide the angle.

Chapter 14:
HUMAN ALLIANCES

Sixteen months since the Hampshire incident

The consulate at night never quite slept; it restlessly rearranged its noises.

Air droned in the vents; server fans ticked like distant cicadas. Cassie had learned to read through the hiss, the same way she read through reports, by weighing where the noise wasn't. Her browser was a nest of tabs: cargo lists, crew manifests, container-yard maps, anonymized duty rosters. Nothing said anything straight. It was all inference and absence.

The burner in her jacket buzzed once. Not the posture-buzz of a spam tree, not the chirp of a wrong-time-zone friend. Purposeful. She let it buzz a second time, picked it up, and answered.

"Reeve."

A man's voice, measured, clipped, no wasted syllables. "You've been watching the port."

She held her breath a beat too long. "Who is this?"

"Look at the paperwork on JG-4127. The man who signed it out hasn't been in Shanghai for six weeks. He's in Hangzhou. But his name still approves night moves." A pause that wasn't hesitation, room for her to decide who he was. "Sloppy work from people who imagine themselves inevitable."

Her chair creaked. She'd found exactly that irregularity at three in the morning, eyes sandpaper-dry, after crosswalking export flags against night-shift attendance. She hadn't told anyone, not even David. "You're guessing."

"No," he said. Short and calm.

She swallowed. "Black."

"You can hang up," Jude said mildly. "When you confirm I'm right, remember who told you."

"Why tell me this?" She kept her voice flat.

"Because the local authorities would rather burn than bend," he said. "And your superiors would rather doubt than move. Between fire and doubt, you, Ms. Reeve, might be the only one left who listens."

She forced her grip to relax. "If you're trying to recruit me, you're terrible at it."

"I don't want you on my side," he said. "I want you alive long enough to stop them."

"Stop who?" She didn't blink.

"You already know," he said, and the line went dead.

She stared at the cheap plastic handset like it might leave a mark. David knocked and leaned in.

"You look like you saw a ghost," he said.

"I heard one," she answered, and slid the phone beneath a stack of printouts. On a fresh page of her field notebook, she wrote, in tidy block letters: *Next time I set the net. And I will still answer.*

She allowed herself one breath, one closed-eye beat of feeling hunted and hunting at once, and then she went back to work. She didn't type "JG-4127." She typed the inspector's name. She pulled shift-change footage. She pinged a contact in Hangzhou with a question that sounded like a favor owed. She checked which cameras on the north fence were on scheduled maintenance and which had been "accidentally" misaligned.

The room hummed. The city outside hummed louder.

Shanghai at night mirrored itself until even the reflections were tired. Ella stood in People's Square as if the city had placed her there to test its angles. Marsten trailed her like a shadow that had opinions.

Across Renmin Avenue, Jude watched them both from a colonnade and dialed.

Ella answered on the second vibration. "Hello?"

"Don't speak," Jude said, not unkindly. "Turn left. Now."

Recognition tightened the line of her mouth. She obeyed, slipping into a narrow lane where laundry sagged on lines and rain had made the steps shine. Marsten overshot, realized, turned, scanned. By the time his gaze found the alley's mouth, Jude had guided Ella down a service stair, across a corridor that smelled like damp paper, and out into a side street where scooters stitched bright threads through traffic.

They met in a room that believed itself to be anonymous. The carpet thick enough to muffle regret, the window looking down on a river pretending to be still.

"What have you done?" Ella's voice was fury balanced on fear. "Since Hampshire, nothing makes sense. You disappear. Your names surface in files that shouldn't touch mine. Adeel feeds the MoD curiosities instead of facts. Then I land and you pull me off the street like we're in a film. Explain it. All of it."

Jude watched neon spill and break on rain-dark asphalt. "There is an organization," he said. "Not a state. Not a cell your committees have a template for. A thing that wears people and borrows their lives. It burrows into agencies, parties, and armies. It replaces choice with direction and calls it order. Hampshire was a door to them, and we walked through it."

"'We.'" She laughed without humor. "You're not an operator, Jude. Since when do you take on syndicates?"

"I don't," he said. "I move before they do." He turned. Let her see the certainty he'd learned to wear. "And I'm already in it. That's the only qualification that matters."

She stepped closer, fists unclenching by force. "I should call someone."

"Then why haven't you?"

Her throat worked. She didn't answer the question he'd actually asked. "Because you sound like you believe it," she said finally, voice lower.

"Because it's true."

He didn't reach for her. He let her decide. She closed the space slowly, initially awkwardly, then with assurance.

She kissed him first, anger turning to heat, the kind born of fear and familiarity tangled. The hotel room's silence absorbed the rest. Clothes fell away without tenderness, each movement carrying the urgency of unasked questions. For a while, they let bodies speak where words could not, a truce carved out of exhaustion and need. When it ended, the quiet felt heavier than before, filled with things neither of them dared to say.

In the white expanse, Vael stepped into view and gripped the bars hard enough to make Jude's skull sing. "*She weakens you. Every softness is a seam. Seams split under pressure.*"

"*She keeps me human,*" Jude responded.

"*Humans die. Empires don't.*"

Jude stared at the ceiling, feeling Ella's hand splayed warm against his chest. "*Empires rot,*" he answered, "*I thought that was the whole point of the Aethero's refusal to bend to the Assembly.*"

Patient silence followed that felt like disapproval dressed as wisdom.

Ella spoke without opening her eyes. "Tell me one true thing. Just one."

He let a breath out. "The man who looks like me is not the same man you went to Hampshire with."

Her fingers twitched, then stilled. "Then I wasn't wrong to come."

"It would have been safer to be wrong."

"I don't like safe anymore," she said, and the corner of his mouth almost moved.

She sat up. Her hair fell forward in a curtain, and she impatiently pushed it back. "Use me. Or don't. But don't lie to me when not lying is an option." She stood. "If this 'Marsten' guy knocks in the next five minutes, you never existed."

"He already believes that," Jude said.

She glared at him and then, against her will, smiled like a secret. "Don't be clever with me, Jude. Save it for the people who deserve it." She buttoned her shirt, gathered her calm, and left without looking back.

He watched the door settle. In the expanse, Vael moved away from the bars. The cage hummed.

They worked three fronts at once and pretended it was one.

With Qiao's pod, Jude wore command like an old coat. He studied their beautifully ugly map—lines between offices and men and meetings, annotated in a crisp hand—and praised it as if he were the only one allowed to point out the flaws. They had a hand in everything that mattered in China. They admired themselves for it. They should have. Their pride made them fast.

"Your position at the ports is strong," Jude said, eyes on the map, voice mild. "Which is why you must treat it as already compromised."

Kareth sat back with the practiced patience of a man saving his speech for a moment that would make it cost more. Skael made a virtue of silence.

Over bitter tea, Qiao tried to seduce Jude with efficiency. "This system prefers a story about order," she said, watching him watch her. "We have learned to write in its language. We write fast."

"Fast breaks when it hits a corner," Jude said. "We need perfect curves."

She smiled properly then. "You speak like someone who has broken things and called it geometry."

He didn't deny it.

Qiao floated a second show of strength at Waigaoqiao. Jude shook his head. "Shift to Yangshan," he said mildly. "Fixed lanes, cleaner manifests. Waigaoqiao is noise; noise hides mistakes and magnifies them." Kareth bristled at the caution. Qiao considered the bridge and the islands and finally nodded. "We move the next cycle." Jude didn't smile. Predictability would be easier to read if you knew what to read for.

With Cassie, he placed needles, not trails. A manifest line adjusted at midnight to a quantity that made sense until you thought about forklifts' maximum lift. A camera nudge so it framed his face once, like a confession. A duplicate invoice quietly paid from an account name that rhymed, barely, with a shell company she'd already flagged in Paris. It was all plausible mischance, unless you were the same kind of stubborn he was.

With the state, he used the habit of states against them. Through a broker in Jing'an—gray hair, expensive shoes, the kind of middleman who lived at the intersection of favors and fees—Jude let slip that a group of locals had embedded in district logistics and were skimming not money but influence. The broker knew exactly whom to tell. The whisper reached the MSS as a question and the PLA as an insult. Both were irresistible.

He arranged time the way some men shuffle cards. A meeting here, a calendared inspection there, a rumor in a room where the rumor would be heard by the man whose job was to ensure rumors never mattered. He never said "warehouse." He said the name of a supervisor's mistress. That was more persuasive than coordinates. The whisper carried a date and weather note that only made sense on the Donghai Bridge.

Vael watched him work and didn't speak for a long time. When he finally did, it was as if he'd been rehearsing and acquitting himself poorly.

"What happens when the stories you tell stop listening to you?" Vael asked.

"Then you tell a stronger one," Jude said.

Vael came close enough within the expanse that Jude could feel him like the weather. *"You balance fires and call it prudence. I have seen more cities than you. I have watched balance become arrogance by inches. You have that look."*

"Do you also have a better plan," Jude asked, *"or just a better insult?"*

Vael's laugh was short and not kind. *"The better plan is not to love. The better plan is to be one blade, not two, fighting for the hilt. I would do differently, but I don't control this body."*

Jude let himself be distracted by the thought of Ella's hand on his chest, passing through him like heat.

Cassie's map of the docks existed in layers no software could render. She had the official schematic, yes: the numbered yards, lanes, cranes, gates, catwalks, camera arcs. But she had built a second map in her head: where the forklifts hesitated at night because the concrete had a slope; where a man named Wu always took his cigarette at 02:10 between Stacks 12 and 14; where the fence had been patched three times by two different contractors and would flex if you leaned just so.

She, Marsten, and their Shanghai liaison sat in a van that looked like it had been parked on that street every night for a year. The cell-site mimic purred quietly, harvesting metadata with clinical patience.

Cassie hated how easily her mind framed the work as dialogue, as if Jude were speaking back with every faint signal, when it should only ever be a hunt.

Two nights later, a different pattern twitched. A convoy request tagged for "routine calibration" appeared on a schedule Cassie had never seen used at night. Destination fields were blank, but the route memo carried a weather note about crosswinds on the Donghai Bridge, a detail that only mattered if the convoy was headed for another port.

"Yangshan," she said to Marsten, tapping the line. "They're shifting." He didn't ask why she sounded certain. He'd learned the shape of her certainty.

Her burner, the cheap one, vibrated once. No call; a text; no reply channel.

21:40—Warehouse 3A. Floodlights glitch north mezz. Watch the shadow line. Main cast will be there.

She showed Marsten. He frowned. "That's him?"

"Yes," she said. "And he wants an audience."

"Are we giving him one?"

"Only the part where we arrest him and his friends," she said, and radioed the consulate: "Movement likely at Yangshan Warehouse 3A. Request deconfliction with locals." The answer took four minutes and said nothing in seventeen words, which meant *we heard you, and no one wants their name on the decision.*

She called David back home. "I'm about to step into something where you'll want credit later and deniability now."

His sigh carried four time zones. "You have a team?"

"A car. Two nerves. We'll borrow the rest."

"You always do," he said, which was either affection or indictment, and hung up.

She adjusted her gun in its holster and tasted metal and saw the night of Paris in her bones and told herself not to miss this time.

Jude closed the laptop on the pod's schematics and opened a different line, one buried three layers under spoofed IDs and burned through towers that would forget they'd ever carried it. The screen resolved into Rakkar's face, pale in the glow of too many monitors back in London.

"You've been quiet," Rakkar said without greeting.

"Quiet keeps us alive," Jude replied. "What have you found?"

Rakkar tilted the camera toward a mess of fractured syntax overlaying financial records. "Signals riding piggyback on trade flows. I think one of the pods we know is trying to write itself into systems we don't control. France had the same fingerprints before Paris. This isn't random, Vael. Someone's improvising."

"Or baiting," Jude said.

Rakkar's jaw tightened. "And if it is, how long before the CIA woman sees the same traces? She's already chasing us from Paris."

"Let her see just enough," Jude said softly. "Just not what matters."

Rakkar didn't like it, Jude could tell. But Rakkar's role was to solve patterns, not rewrite them. That was Jude's task.

The next call was shorter, Sarun's voice crackling through a handset that had no camera.

"Shanghai?" Sarun asked. "Bold choice."

"Necessary," Jude said.

"You're not the only one making moves here," Sarun replied. "I've heard chatter in MoD circles, my kind of chatter. If I can hear it, others can. You're juggling fire."

"That's what keeps the room warm," Jude said.

Sarun laughed, but the sound didn't carry humor. "You'll burn yourself one day, Takra. We can't afford that."

The line went dead without farewell.

Vael shifted against the bars in the expanse, eyes like embers in the dark. "*They smell something. The young one fears betrayal in the code. The sly one fears losing his own place in your design. Both are right to fear.*"

Jude closed the last window and let the silence of the Shanghai night settle around him. He could still hear the river, steady as breath, carrying cargo that didn't care who ruled it.

Tomorrow the trap would spring. Tonight, he measured the cracks in his own house.

Chapter 15: SHANGHAI GAMBIT

The warehouse was a cathedral for boxes. Steel ribs, high windows, a mezzanine that pretended to be a balcony. On the floor, a choreography of machines and hands. The smell of oil and damp cardboard. The sound of weight and men.

Qiao stood with her people near the rail and looked down at an operation that believed itself to be ordinary. Wei carried a tablet he didn't need; he liked the way it let him touch authority. Kareth hovered like an orator looking for a balcony. Skael watched entries, exits, angles. Tom tried, and failed, not to think of how many hands had touched each box. Jude stood between them all like an unmoved point.

"Now," Cassie said into her mic, and the van she was in went from nothing to engine to silent movement. She and Marsten slipped out and started running into the air that smelled like rain remembered.

"Now," a PLA lieutenant whispered, and men with rifles ran along lines that had been measured in a meeting, not in the world.

"Now," said no one in the MSS car because no one in that car used words when watching men with rifles do what bureaucrats had decided to watch.

"Now," Qiao said, and a forklift moved three pallets it wasn't scheduled to move.

The first floodlamps thumped on. The second wave stuttered as if surprised at being asked. Gunfire cracked. A crate splintered into a cloud of false snow. Men shouted in a language of command with the same tone in every country.

Kareth fired at bodies and told himself they were enemies. Skael fired once, then moved, then fired again. Tom raised his gun and lowered it and raised it and chose a cable and shot it down instead of a man; the walkway dipped, and three uniforms hit the floor swearing. Jude took his elbow and turned him, and the bullet that would have carried Tom's name went somewhere else.

Cassie saw a profile at the edge of a flood, the man who was still when all other things shook. She didn't need the name to feel the shape of him. She lined up a shot. He stepped into the darkness like the darkness had been waiting.

On the mezzanine, Qiao made three correct decisions fast and one wrong one faster. She sent two of hers down the stairs that were already held. She pulled Wei back when he would have run directly into the fire. She took one step toward the corner office to cut the feed to the yard and then stopped because she saw the reflection in the glass and understood that the corner office was a net, not a room.

The PLA pushed in twos, men shouting and answering themselves. Cassie's unit cut along the north doors, using stacks of boxes that did not care who won as cover. MSS observed, recorded, and didn't interfere until the interference would look like triumph.

"Out," Jude said, and his voice carried that sculpted calm that made men obey before they were aware of having chosen. He moved them through a door that a foreman would have sworn was for staff only. Down a stair that a designer had placed for no reason he could remember. Into a corridor that ran too long for the building it served. A service hatch. The smell of oil and stale water. The sound of trains on the concrete.

Skael went first. Kareth argued under his breath with no one and resented himself for obeying. Tom-Zherin hesitated at the hatch and then went because Jude put a hand between his shoulder blades and pushed without any force at all.

Behind them, the battle hiccupped, change-of-plan echoing in three languages. Jude's group peeled off through a side stairwell, their silhouettes flickering for a moment in the sodium light. Cassie saw them—Jude at the center, calm even in chaos—and took two steps to follow.

The first shot came from Qiao. Sparks tore from the wall above Cassie's head, plaster dust in her teeth. She dove, rolled, and came up with her Glock already barking. The Aethero woman moved like she'd been trained to move, precise arcs behind crates, answering fire with the cold rhythm of someone who believed the system itself bent around her.

"You can't stop what's already begun," Qiao spat in accented English, reloading with surgical calm.

Cassie's reply was three rounds, the last one finding its mark. Qiao staggered, shock flickering across features too proud for fear, then dropped against the forklift she'd once used as a signal. The machine hissed and settled, a monument to nothing.

Cassie stood over her for half a breath, chest heaving. She should have felt triumph; instead, she felt the seconds slipping away. Jude's group was gone, vanished into rain-slick corridors, ghosts she could never quite corner.

Outside, rain thickened. Inside, light blurred. Sirens arrived late enough to be plausible.

By the time the third wave of men with authority arrived, the pod was ash, the floor was chaos, and the paperwork had started writing itself.

The Zhangjiang lab had also gone to ground, silent, yet intact enough to make a base substrate for someone to get it out of the country if they chose their harbor well.

Cassie holstered her weapon, tasting failure and victory at once, iron on her tongue, smoke in her hair. She wrote the report in her head even as she stood there: calm, reasonable, with no mention of the silhouette she'd almost called by name.

Somewhere in a ministry, a report copied another report and changed the nouns. Somewhere in a party office, a meeting moved twenty minutes, and history pretended it mattered.

Across an ocean, Nireva opened a sanitized cable that said nothing and said everything. She traced the shape of the nothing with her finger on paper, her expression unreadable. If Jude had survived the ambush, it would explain the pattern. If he had orchestrated it, the implications were sharper still. She didn't yet know whether that thought should make her wary or glad. What she did know was that someone had moved pieces others dared not touch. And that meant the game was no longer being played by the rules she'd been given.

When Ella emerged from the bathroom door, the room on the twelfth floor took in the smell of citrus and new sheets. She had showered the smoke out of her hair and put worry under a layer of powder.

She went downstairs and waited in the alley. When Jude arrive, she didn't greet him; she looked at him like he might be the last good or the first bad thing. He moved closer. Their hands found each other because hands learn shortcuts the mind does not.

He told her enough truth to hold for a night. "It's going to look like a rogue cell," he said. "It will be tidied into language that means less than it did before. The wrong men will get credit. The right ones will be replaced. And you will see my name in places it shouldn't be, because that is how this works."

"You think I'm still going back to London to write memos?" she asked, not needing him to answer. "I want in."

His jaw tightened. "You want to be alive."

"I can want both."

Vael hissed in the expanse. "*She will make you choose at the worst moment. She will make you slow.*"

Jude said, "If you're in, you listen. You don't improvise."

"Since when do I improvise?" she asked, and he almost laughed. She moved to him, and he let himself be held. For a minute, they were not chess pieces. For a minute, they were just two people trying not to drown.

In the corridor, a camera watched them for an extra beat and then forgot what it had seen.

Tom-Zherin noticed Jude leaving before Skael did and followed him discreetly. Skael trusted; that was his virtue and his danger. Kareth noticed them both gone and told himself he had not been left behind on purpose. Trust and danger. In that moment, they couldn't think otherwise; for all his shortcomings, Vael had saved them from an ambush yet again.

As he paced, Tom-Zherin told himself he wanted to make sure Vael wasn't walking into a trap. He told himself he wanted to say thank you for the hand on his back that had turned a bullet into a hanging cable instead of himself. He told himself he only wanted to understand why his Takra had started moving in ways the rest of them couldn't follow. Every day it felt more like Vael was carrying a map none of them were allowed to see. Tom-Zherin didn't know where that road ended, only that he was being asked to walk it blind.

He found the passageway because he'd learned how Jude thought about space. He waited until Ella left, eyes big with something that might be hope and might be exhaustion. She didn't see him. He let her go. He breathed once and walked into the alley.

Jude let the shape on his face be neutral. "Zherin."

"In or out," Tom-Zherin said, and stopped because the words that came next felt like betrayal, no matter how he arranged them. "Is she... on our side?"

"Our side," Jude said, and Tom-Zherin hated the way he said it, as if the word were too small now. "She understands the stakes."

Tom-Zherin took that and put it somewhere it wouldn't cut him. "Since when?"

"Since now."

Tom-Zherin nodded, once. The kind of nod men give to lies they want to be truths because truths would break something else. He stepped in. The room held two sets of heat, one fading, one rising.

"Did they all die?" Tom-Zherin asked, the words catching like splinters in his throat.

"Yes," Jude said.

Tom-Zherin looked at the sky because it was easier than looking at Jude's eyes. "I keep thinking about Hampshire," he said. "About the exact second we stopped being only ourselves, I'm not even sure that's the way we should be thinking about what 'ourselves' means. I try to measure it. I can't. I think about the man on the catwalk tonight. I could have shot him. I didn't. Then I shot the cable. I don't know which man that makes me."

"The one who's still deciding," Jude said.

"And is that allowed?" Tom asked, voice breaking on the question. "Do we get to be men who still decide?"

Vael stepped forward in the expanse, and even without words Jude could feel the answer the war wanted to give: "*No.*"

Silence pooled. Tom-Zherin turned, pacing two steps, three, the way people do when they are asking their bodies to tell them what their minds cannot.

"How long has she been in, really?" he asked finally, not turning back, staring at the bland art on the wall as if pictures might tell a truer thing than people.

Jude's hand had already moved to the gun before he knew he had chosen to move. Vael was a pressure in the skull, a cold insistence: "*He will break you, by accident or mercy. Kill him for our survival.*" It wasn't rage. It was math.

"Zherin," Jude said.

Tom-Zherin's right hand shifted toward his jacket. The motion was small, panicked, possibly human. It could mean a gun. It could mean a phone. It could mean a memory he wanted to hold with his fingers just long enough to feel like himself again.

Jude saw a dozen futures at once, and someone he loved died in every one where he waited.

He fired.

The sound was both louder and softer than he expected. Tom-Zherin staggered like a thought had changed under him. He looked at Jude with bewilderment pouring through pain. For a clear bright second the Aethero part seemed to fully recede and the boy he had been stepped forward.

"Are we... back from the hike?" Tom-Zherin asked, dazed, voice young and lost, back against the wall. He swayed, knees loose, lips moving around a word that never came, and then he was on the moss that swallowed sound.

Ella came back because she had forgotten to say something or because the universe liked symmetry. Her breath made a sound like stepping into cold water. She saw what she saw. Jude stood with the gun still in his hand. Tom lay on his side like a man sleeping badly.

"What did you do?" she whispered, and the room understood it was a verdict even if no court would ever hear it.

Jude felt the moment land. In the expanse, Vael said nothing, which was the worst kind of applause.

Jude crossed to Tom's body and knelt and touched the shoulder that had been under his hand in the warehouse. He said his name once, plain and human, as if the sound could hold him a few seconds longer. It was the first time in a long time he could address him as "Tom" and not "Zherin", but it was also the last. He closed Tom's eyes because some gestures are the only ones left.

He stood. He put the gun down very carefully on the ground. He didn't look at Ella when he spoke. "You need to leave," he said, and his voice had that calm that other men mistook for lack of feeling.

"Right now, back to your hotel. Don't speak to anyone at the desk. Don't look back."

"Jude," she said, and he didn't let himself hear whatever word she might have planned to put next.

The white stretched and the cage hummed in the expanse, and Vael watched without pity. "*You chose, Jude. You chose the victory over the man. We have both survived today.*"

Jude didn't answer. He stood at the window and watched Shanghai reflect itself until it looked like a city made entirely of other cities. He put one hand flat against the pane. He felt the cold come through. He didn't move it.

The door opened without warning. Jude stepped inside, rain still beading on his coat, the air shifting as if the room itself had been waiting for him.

Kareth straightened. "You left us."

Jude didn't flinch. "We were being tailed. I took Zherin to peel them away. Better two than four."

Skael's voice was quiet. "And Zherin?"

Jude paused a fraction too long. "He didn't make it through."

The silence that followed wasn't grief, not yet. It was a calculation, each man weighing what the loss meant for the group, for their chances.

Kareth's eyes narrowed. "Convenient. You vanish, he dies, and you return with nothing but your word."

Jude met his stare evenly. "I returned with you still breathing. That's more than he has. Decide whether you want to spend his death second-guessing, or use it to keep moving."

Skael shifted uncomfortably but said nothing. Kareth looked away, jaw tight, his silence not agreement but the kind that promised this wasn't finished.

Outside, the rain thickened. Inside, the air felt thinner than it had before Jude left.

The name Lin Qiao appeared in a list on a screen that meant she would not appear anywhere else for a while. Wei's did not; records of him had vanished between a bullet and paperwork, and likewise Tom's. All security camera footage had also been suspiciously erased and switched off.

The MSS called the operation a success. The PLA counted their brass and wrote letters to families in a tone that pretended duty was a gift. Both refused to cooperate with requests from the CIA for intel sharing. The papers did what papers do.

Cassie wrote her report twice. The first draft said the thing she meant. The second said the thing a committee would read. She sent the second and hid the first in a folder named for a lunch order no one would ever search.

David knocked. "We got anything worth the bruises?"

"Depends who's counting," she said. "Officially? Rogue cell, neutralized by locals. Unofficially? Black played three orchestras at once and made it sound like one song."

"Marsten's going to love that," David said.

"Marsten's going to underline the bits where it sounds like we weren't there. Then he's going to ask me to email him the underlined bits."

"You going to?"

"I'm going to send him a photograph," she said, and slid across the still, a man's profile half-caught in a glitch of light, the angle wrong for face-recognition and perfect for memory. "Because next time, I'm not going to be in the wrong doorway."

She added one more line to her notebook: *He calls. I don't answer. I'm already there.*

Jude sat alone for a long time after the window stopped feeling like ice. He unmade the expanse by refusing to go there. Eventually, he slept with his eyes open, which is a trick you learn if you don't have a better one.

When he woke, the city had reset into morning. He wrote three messages and didn't send them. He called one number and hung up before it rang. He looked at the gun on the table for long enough that it started to look like a tool, which it was, and not a decision, which it had also been.

Vael came close. "*You will tell yourself it was necessary. You will be right. You will tell yourself it was the only path. You will be wrong. There was a second path for a second longer than you allowed.*"

"*I know,*" Jude said.

"*You will survive because you will choose the first path faster next time.*"

"*I know,*" Jude said again, and the answer was not pride.

He stood, put on the jacket he wore when he needed to look like a man who got what he wanted by asking nicely, and left the room that still contained the shape of a body.

The city outside did not care. That was one of the reasons he liked it.

He met Ella one last time before departure, in a café where coffee tasted of burned sugar and relief. She wore a hat pulled low and a face that belonged to someone else.

"I'm leaving," she said.

"I know."

"You're not going to tell me where you're going."

"No."

She traced the rim of her cup with a finger and then looked up and said, as if casually, "Am I on your side?"

He let himself answer without checking with the part of him that kept score. "You're on the side that matters," he said. "Your own. Keep it intact."

"Don't patronize me," she said, and smiled the smallest possible smile. "Tell me one thing I can do that will make a difference."

"Keep breathing," he said. "And when you read words that smell like disinfectant, remember that I was not in the room."

She nodded. "And Tom," she said, finally, and the name slid across the table and lay between them.

"He was my friend," Jude said. The sentence did not contain all of it. But it was the truth.

She stood, gathered her bag, and said, "If you break yourself on this, I will be very angry."

"I'm good at not breaking," he said, and she gave him a look that said *you're lying* and left.

He watched her go. He let himself watch her turn the corner and not come back.

The plane they took out did not belong to Tom's uncle. It belonged to a shell that belonged to a shell that belonged to an idea, a remnant of Qiao's hospitality for her British guests. Kareth stared out the oval window and rehearsed speeches that sounded like history. Skael read nothing and learned more from it. Jude closed his eyes and made a list of the next doors to open and the men to station at them.

When the wheels left the runway, Shanghai turned into a model of itself. The river drew a line. The docks looked like a child's game with pieces removed.

In the expanse, the white room held steady. Vael stood at the bars and watched him without blinking.

You will pay for every mercy, the Aethero general said.

"I already am," Jude said, and the city fell away.

PART IV:

PRESSURE FRONT

Chapter 16:
ENCROACHMENT

Jupiter turns like a slow machine, its storms taller than mountains, folding and re-folding around a red eye that has watched longer than anything human.

Across that patient violence, a shadow drifts vast, deliberate, then slows to near stillness.

Something immense. Bio-mechanical. Flanked by smaller monoliths of the same design. They carry no beacons, emit no signals, bleed only enough heat to pass for stone.

Through a human telescope, they would be nothing more than noise. They spoke little. In war, silence is not an absence. It is a posture.

Earth spins blue and white, unaware.

Jude lay awake in the safehouse, the air conditioner's hum a pale imitation of what he imagined a ship's white noise might sound like. When he closed his eyes, the expanse unraveled not into cages, but into a memory that wasn't his.

Aethrie.

In the Aethero tongue, the word carried a gravity of its own. Not ship. Not planet. Something between. A world the size of a moon, hauled across the stars by engines older than their rebellion. A fortress bound in armor, anchored by vast pillars that reached into its surface. A prison that had learned to dream of freedom, a dream forty million Aethero shared.

At its heart pulsed the Core. A substance denser than anything catalogued, bending gravity into Earth-like strength, radiating a magnetic shield against the void. No one alive understood it. No one dared. The Core was worshiped, feared, and preserved. Their lives orbited it as faithfully as Aethrie orbited the stars.

Above the habitat layer stretched the shell kilometers of alloy, scarred by millennia, lined with thrusters and weapons left by hands long dead. No Aethero could replace them. They could only patch, coax, and pray. To damage the shell was to risk annihilation. To harm the Core was to invite extinction. Jude saw fragments the way a man sees lightning through shutters.

The inner sanctums, children drilling in formation before they could even spell their own names.

Hydroponic caverns, tiered in steel and light, where crops grew beneath lamps older than memory.

Cathedral-hangars where fleets nested like birds around a single indestructible egg.

There were no oceans. Water was cut into shapes, rectangles, channels, and mirrored squares. Function before beauty. The land itself felt engineered: precise, geometric, like the interior of a weapon. Crops rose in strict terraces under domes of calculated light. Housing blocks loomed in grids, severe and dark, their order treated as faith. To live there was to be reminded daily that survival was not given, but drilled.

Forty million souls endured beneath that controlled sky. Generations sealed in fusion glow had stripped variety down to muted tones. Blue marks bloomed on their skin, neither decoration nor invention, but inheritance. Radiation's constant bite had bent chemistry itself, shifting melanin until pigment streaked like tattoos gifted by evolution. Even in memory, it looked less like biology and more like belief written into flesh. Soldiers and workers bent to their tasks. Children drilled to march before they could run. A people raised on the same creed for millennia: we endure because our masters failed to break us, and endurance will not always be enough. One day, they were told, endurance would give way to conquest. One day, they would claim a world of their own, neither borrowed nor mechanical, but alive.

Yet beneath the ritual chants and the soldier's cadence lay the truth Vael never dared speak aloud. Aethrie was failing. A giant running on half-forgotten equations, held together by engineers who repeated patterns they no longer fully understood. The fusion core still burned clean, but with each decade it demanded more ore, more sacrifice, more drift through system after system just to keep the lights alive.

Every raid, every expedition, every generation had been taught the same refrain: this is the march to a new home.

And yet, after a hundred thousand years, home had never come. The Assembly had tightened its grip on every corridor of drift, closing routes one by one until Aethrie's path was little more than scavenger trails.

The Assembly never struck them outright. And the Aethero, in turn, preyed only on the weak border colonies, derelict stations, and settlements that could be stripped without waking giants. Both sides understood the same truth: a full war would be a war of attrition, and neither could afford it.

Then came Earth. A shimmer in the archives, stolen from Assembly files. Coordinates. A habitable world with a civilization still primitive enough to be bent, broken, or remade. In the expanse, Vael stirred.

"You see why we cannot turn back. We were born beneath steel ceilings. We prayed to metal walls and called it sky. We will not stop until we touch soil again."

Jude exhaled, slow and quiet. He thought of his family. Of Ella. Of Cassie sprinting through cities where shadows outnumbered truths. And he thought of the world-ship itself, forty million lives clenched together, pressing their weight across the stars like a fist too old to unclench.

If Earth was destiny to them, then to him it was a countdown.

Twenty-five months since the Hampshire incident

Cassie keeps paper on the walls because databases can be rewritten by men who don't like being wrong. The bones of a thing are harder to alter once you've pinned them.

Her office isn't what television promises. No glass walls, no skyline view. The ceiling tile above her chair has a chip missing that she's grown oddly fond of. She has two good chairs and one bad one, the bad one reserved for visitors who make the wrong joke first.

David arrives with coffee and the weathered face of a man who has perfected the trick of looking tired before anyone else can point it out. He sets a file down so gently it still manages to make a sound.

"Your Paris prisoner is still a problem," he says. "Ranting about birthright, about taking back what was ours. We're calling it what everyone calls it when they want the noise to stop."

"Unhelpful?" Cassie asks.

"Unfundable," he corrects. "People higher up like problems they can point at. They don't like a map of something you can't see."

Cassie draws three red circles that touch but don't overlap. Jude Black. Michael Ashworth. Then she adds Lionel Smith, Nathan Doyle, Adeel Shah, Thomas Albright—and marks *'deceased'* against the last. The circles resemble molecules.

"Right-wing cells don't write procurement calendar metadata into contractor APIs," she says, more to the wall than to him.

David watches, not smiling. For him, that's trust.

"If you need a car, take the grey one. If you need a room, pick one no one else would."

"I'll need both," she says.

"And if you're wrong?"

"I'll be specific about why."

He nods, once. That's their bargain. He is the phone call. She is the map.

Upstairs, someone calls down to say they've scheduled a Monday briefing and already half-apologized for the time they'll waste. Cassie thanks them, then forgets. Monday is far away when your world runs in fifteen-minute jumps.

At lunch, she eats a granola bar standing, frowning at a logistics report that moved a hearing by twelve minutes. Too boring to notice, too specific to ignore. No one shifts a hearing by twelve minutes unless a decision was made the week before and buried. She writes it down. The dullest irregularities often tell more than the flashy ones.

She does not think about the stars. Her enemies breathe the same air, bump shoulders in the same corridors, drink coffee from the same machine, lie on the same forms with different pens. They are close sometimes, too close.

But for months now, the trail of Jude Black and the others had gone cold. Their signals buried too deep, scrubbed too clean. The silence gnawed at her.

She heads to Union Station to meet Marsten, a place that eats faces the way rivers eat cities; loud, endless, forgetful. Cassie pauses midstream because something catches her eye: a posture, the tilt of a head, a stride too practiced in looking like nothing.

"Black," she whispers.

She doesn't sprint. Sprinting makes security look up. She slides. Marsten reads her and follows, two fish parting and recombining in the current. For a second, she has him. For a second, she sees how he'll take the escalator instead of the stairs, letting a tide of tourists with rolling suitcases cut her off.

An ambulance siren shrieks through the glass, tilting the acoustics. She clears a family whose matriarch is scolding someone in Spanish over the wrong bag, and the man is not him.

Marsten doesn't say next time, or doubt she even saw him. Paris taught him better. He just breathes, once, and looks at her.

"You were right," he says. Which, from him, is an apology.

"He wants me to know it," Cassie replies. Not arrogance. Reading. "He's making sure I'm in the room when they move next."

"Do we want to be?" Marsten asks.

"We don't get to choose." She files a time and place into memory, where no paper can lose it.

The clapboard house in northern Virginia looks like a thousand others stamped onto the grid, twenty minutes from a metro line. The porch sags an inch past code. The mailbox tilts. The grass tries to go feral and fails. No one on the street could describe its occupants without sounding guilty.

Inside: a table that wobbles unless you press the right corner, a whiteboard polished nearly clear by erasure, three prepaid phones in a ceramic bowl, two laptops warming the air with the smell of plastic. Five people learning the art of being ordinary.

Skael becomes the metronome. He repeatedly cleans the same pistol at the window with the narrowest view of the street. Strips it to spring and screw. Reassembles blindfolded. Wipes each part with a cloth that never seems to get dirty. He times himself but never records it. The point isn't speed. The point is that ritual ends the same way every time in a world that doesn't.

Kareth wears a track into the hall, back and forth, back and forth. He doesn't shout at neighbors, but his voice still cuts, a blade wrapped in a towel. "We are wasting position," he says, often. "Waiting is for men who have already lost." He sketches seizures in the air with his hands: this office, that function, the shape of a strike. Even asleep on the narrow couch, boots aligned, his jaw works like he's still arguing.

Rakkar is the hum beneath everything. He builds defenses inside the laptop balanced on a chopping board because the kitchen table shorts the charger bare. He calls them gates, with the weight of prayer. His code is clean. His notes, messy. His words come in bursts.

Sarun brews tea. He has opinions about kettles and water temperature that exist mostly to pass the time. He smiles when the doorbell rings, puts the smile away before opening. Delivery men like him which is useful. Receptionists like him, which is how two building passes went missing and came back with scuff marks unnoticed.

Jude moves as though the house were an instrument only he can tune. He rotates cars and stores, routes and routines, swaps phones before their batteries admit they're dying. He has rules for breaking rules and a rule against saying them aloud. He listens when Kareth talks and nods in places that mean nothing. He tells Rakkar which logs to burn, which to salt. He lets Sarun believe the joke was his idea.

After two months of motels, long-distance buses, and the streaked blur of interstates since arriving in the U.S. with Nireva's help, they lived the last five months this way. They learned the sound of the postman's knock, different from the utility contractor's, different again from the rare neighbor with misplaced flyers. They tensed when the dog next door barked at the wrong hour, a short, startled bark instead of the bored chain that filled most afternoons. Skael checked the window. Jude raised a finger. No one breathed.

That was survival's shape: not heroics, but a life starved down to safe calories.

When night came, it came in two versions. Outside, the ordinary darkness of a suburb counting down to trash day. Inside Jude's head, a white space with bars, and the sound of a hand that kept testing them.

"*You are letting them rust,*" Vael said.

"I am keeping them alive," Jude answered.

"Soldiers rot when they are not tested."

"Dead soldiers don't argue."

The bars shook as if a punch had landed and missed bone.

Jude kept breathing, because breath was the only thing Vael couldn't yet take from him.

Chapter 17: SEEDING

On the wrong days, the Capitol glows like a target. On the right days, it looks exactly as it was designed to: a building where process pretends to be destiny.

Jennifer Graves keeps her office in one of the duller corridors. That is no accident. She knows the ratio of cameras to corners. She knows which elevators break and which "break." She knows how to look like someone who belongs entirely inside the small rituals of staff meetings and constituent calls.

Behind the heavy door, with the overheads off and the desk lamp burning like a theatre cue, she becomes the other name she carries, the one she only lets herself think in when the cameras are gone: Nireva.

She angled the folder toward Jude as though it were a blade disguised as stationery. Slowly, deliberately, as if even the weight of paper might cut if set down too fast.

The sheaf inside looked like failure at first glance: low-value requisitions, decimals split across pages, vendor codes tied to agencies no one bothered to speak of. To the untrained eye, it was an administrative graveyard of forgotten budgets. To her, it was a skeleton key.

"This is not a lab the way you imagine," she said. "Not a place where white coats dream up cures. Nebraska is both less and more. On paper, it's an arms depot long emptied, a shell meant to house machines no one remembers ordering. The irony is that we will bring machines far beyond anything those walls were built to hold." She tapped the binder once with a fingernail. "Inside, it is also production. Cultivation. Kareth, restless from his lack of action, raised a brow. "You've managed to reproduce the vaccines?"

She leaned back, eyes narrowing as though tracing the memory. "After Shanghai broke, I sent a team into the rubble. Not soldiers, not martyrs, but scavengers. Engineers with enough nerve to walk through a scene the MSS thought they owned. They lifted what they could: sealed cultures, half-burned recipes, a substrate plant that hadn't cracked. Barely a skeleton. But they rebuilt it. Quieter. Smaller. Hidden beneath the noise of Pudong's container traffic."

She allowed herself the smallest smile, all teeth concealed. "It worked. They're finishing their first true batch now, five million doses, enough to make Nebraska worthwhile. Those crates are already booked to sail west. No one will question a few extra containers leaving Yangshan, not when the manifests read like feed additives and precision valves."

Kareth exhaled like a man watching a flag rise. "Five million. An army fit to breathe the same air as its enemy."

Jude's hand tightened on the back of a chair, knuckles whitening. It felt like a retreat to him, like watching a machine shrink from empire to salvage, forced to live off scraps. He said nothing.

But in the white expanse, Vael stirred. His voice moved like heat along iron: *"Resourceful. Even cornered, Nireva carves tools from bone. That is why we Aethero endure."*Nireva went on as if she hadn't noticed the silence between them. "Nebraska is not a new invention. It is multiplication. The seed comes from Shanghai, battered but alive. The soil is here. We graft the two. And when the first shipments move inland, no one will dare open them. They'll believe it's old ordnance, waiting to be destroyed. That is how you move life under the guise of death."

Her eyes flicked up to Jude, sharp. "And this time, it is not theory. It is a calendar."

He nodded.

"We also have hands in places that pretend not to be part of government," she said. "Two primes and a boutique built to say it isn't. They change badges and passwords when asked. They set agendas that look like other people's ideas. A staff director moves a meeting by a few minutes, and a phenomenon occurs: decisions without names find their way onto paper. A weapons pilot project becomes a line-item for rural development. The paper never calls it what it is."

Nireva's aide, someone from the US pod who had been quiet too long for his measure, smiled and leaned in. "Seat a general next to a lobbyist, and policy writes itself before dessert."

"Later," Jude said. Not a rebuke, but a shelf. He added the word he repeats to this network like a steady beat: "Corridors. Not headlines."

Nireva closed one folder and opened another. Corridors were hers. Headline people get caught; corridor people stay.

She did not speak the part that tasted of vanity even in her own mouth: that she enjoyed being again in a place where her hand on a minor lever could move a major door. That she had been writing in this city's lexicon long enough to think in clauses, riders, and staff notes. She kept quiet, knowing how pride smells to a man like Vael: either noise or weapon, if kept sharp.

When they left, the table held two stacks: one labeled with something boring, one with nothing at all. She tucked her human name back onto her shoulders and walked into a hall built to swallow people, not because it tried, but because that was its function. In the wrong light, every corridor here looks like a target. She walked it anyway.

Ella sits through a reception that has more glass than conversation. She has learned to perform the kind of politeness that is both a screen and a blade. Her badge reads *Political Attaché*. What it really means is junior slot: half diplomat, half listener, always close enough to hear, never close enough to shape. By her second week, she stopped drinking at these events; it was easier to carry a glass and appear as if she were on her first.

An aide from the Interior tells her a story about a conference in Denver, framed as one about budget priorities. A man selling drones tries to sell his vision of the future. Two women from Commerce talk about ports with the zeal of converts. Ella nods and nods, storing the names behind the names. She lets her accent work for her the way Americans let their suits.

Across the room, Jennifer Graves is composed in a way that reads as power, not calm. Ella watches her, not because she suspects anything specific, but because the congresswoman radiates the same gravity Jude always had at a table. People bend over their drinks and leave believing they had the idea first.

Her colleagues at the Embassy are polite to her face and puzzled when she's not there. She has a desk near a window and a badge that opens fewer doors than it should. It is an annoyance she wears like a reminder not to blunder.

At home, in a rented apartment that smells faintly of paint and the last tenant's detergent, she keeps the Hampshire photos in a folder she moves to the bottom of her home screen every week and then drags back up again. They look like a lie now. People in jackets under trees, cheeks pink from wind and beer. A man who looks like Jude, but isn't, smiling with body language that doesn't carry an agenda.

When the burner in her handbag vibrates against the table leg, she answers without saying hello.

"Public distance," Jude says. The line feels like a tightrope stretched between two rooftops.

"Private precision," she answers, because they've made a game of matching phrases.

"You look well," he says after a breath. It is an odd thing to risk a call for.

Ella looks at the shadow of herself in the window. "I look like someone who knows what the word 'liaison' actually means."

"Stay boring," he says.

"You first."

She wants to ask if he is safe. She wants to ask if he sleeps. She wants to say Tom's name and see if silence falls differently over it than any other word. Instead, she says, "If you need me to open a door, don't ask me to do it blind."

The line clicks soft. He is gone.

She leaves the phone on the counter and tells herself she is not the kind of woman who waits at windows. Outside, a siren winds past, as if the city has lungs that need to clear.

The call happens at two in the morning because that is the hour when fear quiets enough to let someone dial a number they've been staring at for months.

"Jude?"

Naomi's voice snaps something in his chest that the last two years had hardened into habit. The ceramic bowl of phones sits on the counter. He has swapped SIMs, moved to the back bedroom, and stood by the window where the neighbor's porch light doesn't quite reach. It still feels too loud.

"It's me," he says, and the room remembers a different decade for a second.

"Where are you?" Her words trip, then fall. "No one says anything. Mum keeps pretending she's fine and then doesn't look at the kettle while it boils. Dad's doing that thing where he calls secrecy an 'obligation to the public' and not an excuse. People ask me if you're ill. People ask me if you're in trouble. People ask me if you're dead. I've run out of ways to say I don't know."

"I'm alive," he says. It lands like a stone.

"Are you safe?" she asks, and that is harder.

"I'm not in the hospital," he says, which is not an answer.

"Is Tom with you?" Naomi pushes. "Leo? Mike? You all just..."

"We're together," he lies. "We had to go quiet."

"Why?" She whips the word at him. "I am your sister. You don't get to..." She tries to say *control*. What comes out is *abandon*.

He closes his eyes and sees a warehouse floor in Shanghai, light smeared by rain, the way a man he loved like a brother fell in an instant none of them had rehearsed.

"If I give you the truth," he says quietly, "you won't sleep again this year."

"You think I sleep now?" Naomi says, and there's the part he recognizes: the sharpness that made her un-bully-able at school, the one that made their father think twice before bringing work home in the shape of opinions. "Look after them," he says. "Don't let them break."

"I can't keep lying," she says. "I'm rubbish at it."

"You're better than you think," he replies, and hates himself.

There's a silence where she could say don't you dare ask me to cover for you. She fills it with breath instead. "Please come home," she says, and it isn't an order, so he can't not obey it.

"I'll try," he says, and the lie almost chokes him.

He doesn't move for a long time when the line goes dead. The house creaks. A car passes with a bassline too big for its frame. He sets the phone back in the bowl as if returning a knife to a drawer.

From the hall, a floorboard shifts. Skael is there, leaning in the doorway, eyes sharp, measuring. He doesn't bother to hide that he's been listening. Jude meets his gaze and gives a single nod—clipped, mechanical, the way Vael would. Skael holds the stare a moment longer, then turns away without a word. That is the language now: not trust, not friendship, but performance. Enough to survive the next hour.

Days stretch into errands with teeth.

Sarun practices his trade: getting people to offer him things they normally wouldn't. He prints a set of conference name tags on a lost printer, then uses them to enter a breakfast where a deputy under-secretary lectures on "modernization" in the passive voice. He leaves with a cheap pen and a story that lets him walk into a different building later and act as if he belongs. He does belong; that is the trick.

Skael tails a courier three blocks longer than the route merits. He doesn't step on the man's shadow; he counts the cameras. He notes which door the pouch goes through, which it emerges from, and who signs once and doesn't sign a second time.

Rakkar shows Jude a dashboard built of loops that don't know they're loops. "Calendar fields hitching a ride on vendor endpoints," he says. "It's like teaching bad code to wear a suit. I can make it blink if I push here." He presses a key. Somewhere, a line of numbers falters. Somewhere else, a door fails to open on the first pass of the keycard and opens on the second.

Jude runs a finger along the table's edge until the splinter that always catches him smooths. "Don't pull the whole thread," he says. "Just enough that I can see where it leads

Nireva finagles a hearing into being twelve minutes longer than anyone planned. Twelve minutes is a lot when it sits at the right point in the agenda. The extra time forces a witness to speak two paragraphs that were never meant to leave his notes. That disclosure pulled a Thursday meeting forward to Tuesday. Someone calls someone else who was going to be in the wrong city on Thursday and is now available on Tuesday. Dominoes aren't always big things. Sometimes they're a chair that didn't squeak because someone oiled it.

Jude calls that progress. Kareth calls it hiding. They don't fight about it yet. They will.

It happens at midnight in a parking garage that smells of hot dust and old oil, because that is where men go in this city when they want to pretend they are not being listened to.

Kareth does not slouch. He stands opposite Jude like a line drawn across concrete. Skael is there because Jude is careful, and because a conversation that starts with posture can end with someone leaving on a stretcher.

"We command," Kareth says, tone fixed and unyielding. "We do not petition. We have set the table for other men's dinners long enough."

"We outlast," Jude answers. "We don't declare."

"You have us drawing maps," Kareth spits, disgust curdling the last word. "We are not cartographers."

Jude steps closer, exactly one step. "We are alive," he says. "That is the job."

Kareth stares a second too long, then looks away, knowing that if he stares longer, the job becomes something else. He leaves first, boots hitting the ramp with a rhythm that thinks it is a drumline. Skael watches him go, then glances at Jude.

"He's right about one thing," Skael says.

"Which one?"

"We need a win that feels like one."

Jude nods. "We will get one that looks like boredom on paper and keeps the other kind of win possible."

Skael almost smiles. "You do know how to sell a night out."

It is late. The building is empty enough that footsteps sound like confessions.

Nireva had three files open across her desk, each carrying coded numbers that looked harmless to an untrained eye. She tapped one page with her pen.

"These shipments will be flagged by Commerce in two weeks unless we nudge the audit schedule. A minor adjustment, nothing visible."

Jude leaned against the doorframe instead of sitting. "And when they see the containers?"

"They won't," she replied. "They'll see manifests. Paper beats metal when the right hands are moving it."

He stepped closer, eyes on the lines she had drawn. "Shift the lot forward. A week earlier. That way, the crates pass through the backlog unnoticed."

"That increases exposure," she said, sharper than intended.

"That increases invisibility," he countered, quiet, almost weary. "Inspection teams don't look closely when they're already drowning."

She studied him for a long moment. He didn't flinch, didn't smile, didn't sell it, just laid the sabotage down as if it were logistics. At last, she marked the margin with her pen, expression unreadable.

Jude turned away before she could ask why it mattered so much to him.

"You erode what we build," Vael said inside the white place, voice edged with steel. *"Paris, Shanghai, now here. Each cut weakens the blade."*

Then softer, almost grudging: *"And yet you do it with a precision my own captains would envy. Cunning in betrayal is still cunning. Perhaps I chose well."*

Jude let a corner of his mouth curve in humor at the thought.

Rakkar shows it to Jude after midnight because that is when numbers talk to people who listen.

"It's nothing you can brief," he says, preface first. "It's a feeling with math on it." He flips between public telemetry feeds, ugly and honest, the kind that send raw spew into the world and hope clever people wrap it in graphs later. There is a jitter in the data where there shouldn't be. It is not a machine failing. It is a machine reacting.

"You think?" Jude says.

"I think," Rakkar answers. "I can't prove. Yet."

"Don't try," Jude says. "Not here."

Rakkar looks at him and sees that denial is a kind of confirmation. He shuts the laptop, not because he is afraid anyone might hear, but because he knows when to stop poking a bruise.

In the expanse, the bars sing. Vael is not psychic; he is a soldier whose bones were set in battle. He knows the shape of the drum when it is still muffled, waiting to be struck.

"We are close," he says. It is not triumph. It is the alertness a hunter wears when the wind changes.

Jude doesn't answer at first. He lets the silence work on him like pressure, not pain. When he finally speaks, it is half out loud, in a room with no audience.

"We tighten first," Jude says, and leaves the word *we* hanging, as if it belonged to someone Vael couldn't quite name.

Outside, the porch light across the street clicks on, then off. Somewhere far away, past the clouds, mechanical monoliths adjust their attitude by a fraction of a degree, and no one on the planet notices.

The house settles as if it wants to be forgotten. The people inside practice being the kind of quiet that doesn't feel like defeat.

Jude lies down on the couch Kareth uses for pretending to nap, and for a moment lets the word *family* mean something that isn't a liability. Naomi will sleep badly tonight. Ella will not sleep. Cassie will pin one more note to a wall. Nireva will drink the drink she poured and didn't touch. Skael will finish one more cleaning run and put the pistol away with a click that has become a lullaby. Sarun will wash the mugs because it is the only job left at midnight that looks like care. Rakkar will lie on his back and watch the ceiling, finally talking himself into believing he has not imagined the numbers.

Up beyond the belt, where sensors don't bother to stare, the three shadows fly past the solar system's planetary orbits.

Destination: *Earth.*

Chapter 18:
DROP

Rakkar felt it first as a change in the noise.

He'd left the laptop open on Jude's kitchen chopping board, power cabled through the wood so the charger wouldn't short on the table's metal legs. The dashboard he'd built was ugly and honest: raw telemetry streams, municipal air-traffic slop, a few amateur radio relays piggybacked where no one looked twice, and a narrow-band slice that shouldn't have contained anything at all. It moved.

He leaned in. The house was quiet, the way safe things pretend to be. Kareth paced along a track worn into the carpet, boots whispering. Sarun had gone out to "fetch rice," which could mean anything from groceries to a person. Jude stood in the doorway, a silhouette with a phone in one hand and a rulebook unwritten in the other.

"There," Rakkar said. He didn't point. He lifted the laptop and turned it so Jude could see.

Two short pulses, an empty four-second span, then a longer one that decayed like a bell in a vacuum. A pause that felt deliberate. Then again. It wasn't pretty. It didn't need to be. The shape in the data did what shapes do when meant for someone particular: it ignored the world and asked for an answer.

"It's clean?" Jude asked.

"As clean as anything that crosses three agencies and four hobbyists," Rakkar said. "But the signature is," He stopped himself from saying beautiful. "It's ours."

"Recon," Vael said inside Jude's skull, a low chord that vibrated bone. *"Three crafts. Signal is the old cadence; we used it before the stop-over at Anath. It tells friends to stop looking and start receiving.*

Rakkar's fingers danced. "Origin vector puts the handoff over the Midwest. The quiet patch is a dead drop for location. If you fold it the way we did the European satellite chain," he worked; the numbers resolved. "Nebraska."

Kareth stopped pacing. "Open country. Few eyes."

"Nireva," Jude said, "they've guided them to the lab."

He scrolled to the number labeled with the kind of alias that would look like spam if anyone else saw it and pressed call.

"Congresswoman Graves," Nireva answered, voice flat with the hour, the room, the expected lie.

"We saw the signal," Jude said, as if reporting the weather. "If you were planning to pleasantly surprise me, you have."

A fraction of silence. "Good," she said. "You'll be unsurprised to hear the shipments are already forward."

"That was fast," Jude said.

"You asked me to move them," she replied. "So I moved them."

Kareth turned his head just enough to let the conversation pass under his jaw like a train. Rakkar watched the waveform on the laptop warm and cool, and warm again.

"Important cargo," Jude said. "We'll need eyes there. And hands. Escort them to Nebraska, where you and I will be."

"I'm sending three of mine," Nireva said. "They'll pick up at the port and ride the truck in."

"Which port?" Jude asked.

"Los Angeles," she said. "The maritime traffic was kind to us."

"Kareth and Skael will shepherd it too," Jude said. "I'll see you in Omaha."

"Sounds intimate," she said, and hung up before he could decide whether he liked the way she said it.

Kareth was already in motion, checking a bag that had been examined enough times to wear a groove into the zipper's teeth. "Finally," he said. "Work that isn't typing."

Skael didn't need telling. He closed the top of the pistol he had been cleaning as if tucking a child into bed. He nodded once to Jude. That was their language.

When the door shut behind them, Rakkar touched the laptop, and the signal obediently flared again. "They're on the ground now," he said. "If the cadence means what I think it does."

"It means 'clear,'" Vael said. *"It means 'come.'"*

Jude looked at the numbers and saw not numbers but rails. If he didn't move on them, someone else would. He looked at Rakkar. "Pack it."

"I'm going to Nebraska too?" Rakkar asked, though he'd already started to coil cables.

"We're all going to Nebraska," Jude said. "Just from different directions."

He waited until Rakkar left the room, then slid a second phone toward himself and typed a message with his thumb without looking at the keys: *Port of LA. Tuesday night. Calibrations convoy mislabeled as vet supplies. Warehouse cross-dock 17, Terminal Island.*

He pressed send. Cassie's phone beeped.

Then, he wrote another message on a different app with simpler grammar, and the local authorities were alerted.

"You sharpen the same knife twice," Vael said. "They will feel for the hand that holds it."

"They already do," Jude said. "I'm just making sure they feel the right direction."

The flight to Eppley Airfield carried the same night smells as all red-eyes: coffee old enough to be suspicious, plastic that had held something new for a week and would never feel new again, the fatigue of people who talked louder than they meant to because the altitude made everyone think of being alone.

Nireva met them at the car, without the aide who usually absorbed her edges. She didn't waste sentences.

"Facility is a decommissioned agricultural warehouse southwest of Papillion, retasked as a robotics testing site on paper," she said. "No signage. No one wants to admit they don't know what it is."

"Nobody ever does," Jude said.

Rakkar rode in the back with the laptop balanced on his knees, the glow cutting a line along his cheek. He watched for the signal again out of habit. It wasn't there. That was fine. Signals aren't for the people who show up on time.

The road folded away into fields that had not yet decided which crop to be. The facility looked like the sort of place that imagined a future where no humans would do the work they were about to do. The gate guard waved them through with a badge scanner that blinked once, offended at being used.

Inside, the lead engineer was waiting, carrying an energy that had too much relief in it to be purely professional. He had the earnest face of a man who thought the future could be built with better aluminum. Human. His badge read ERIC HANSEN. His shirt suggested he hadn't slept.

"You got here fast," he said to Nireva, as if it were a compliment he had been holding for years. "It's, well. It's something."

He keyed them through a second door into cool, dry air that smelled faintly of ozone and new rubber. The space beyond was a warehouse in shape and cathedral in intention: high ceiling, white light, three bays cordoned by short metal fences.

In each bay, a craft rested like the idea of a ship made domestic, a room-sized cylinder with muscles hinted at beneath armor, seams that were not seams until you knew to look for them, surfaces broken by ports like gills that opened and closed with the patience of machines that had traveled far and believed they had earned the right to breathe when they wanted to.

Their design gave Jude flashbacks of the Hampshire pod.

"Recon craft," Hansen said, as if translating. "We didn't know until they were almost down. We got the handshake, and the fireteams got the memo at the same time. We chose not to shoot at the things we didn't understand."

"Healthy instinct," Jude said.

Hansen pointed with a pen, because engineers like to keep their hands busy even when they are showing off. "Each carried two, so six arrived in total. They prefer to remain inside, pressure differences, acclimation curves, whatever their doctrine is. We've dosed five of them, as we only had five vials before the first large shipment arrives."

"Great," Nireva said. "Anyone we can meet?"

He pointed to Bay One.

"That's where the active one is," he said. "The second bay is where four are resting. Third, that's where the sixth is, the unvaccinated one." He lowered his voice, as if volume could communicate respect.

"They're larger than I expected."

"They're wearing suits," Nireva said.

"Yes, but even so," Hansen said, flushing as if he'd said something impolite.

The container yard smelled of rust and diesel, the air too heavy for the hour. Cassie sat low in the van's passenger seat, the glow of a laptop screen painting her cheekbones in pale light. The feed stuttered once, then steadied: cranes arched like skeletons, rows of steel containers stacked so high they looked like buildings.

"Three signatures," Marsten whispered from the back, hunched over the scanner. His accent was clipped, precise. "Moving east, lane twelve. They don't belong to any manifest."

Cassie lowered the binoculars and fixed on the dark shapes crossing between the stacks. The men moved with the careful gait of people pretending to be ordinary. Too careful. Their shoulders betrayed them.

"Confirm?" she asked.

Marsten tapped the handheld once. "Armed."

Her pulse climbed a notch. She didn't need confirmation. She already knew.

She slid the earpiece in. "Go."

The van's doors cracked open. Two LAPD detectives in plainclothes spilled out first, weapons low, flanked by a pair of Port Police officers who knew the docks better than anyone. Cassie followed, boots hitting concrete with a muted slap. The night carried sound in strange ways here, metal clanging, gulls crying, the hiss of some distant container door rolling open.

They moved. Shadows within shadows. Backup was not far behind; she was surprised by how fast this operation was resourced.

Lane twelve opened like a throat. A truck idled halfway down, its cab dark but engine running. A shipping container sat skewed on a trailer, doors cracked wide enough for someone to slip in or out.

Cassie lifted a hand. The team froze.

Movement.

The man she knew as Lionel Smith stepped out first, lean frame drawn tall, pistol in hand. Behind him, Michael Ashworth and three others—Americans, but with the same practiced coldness. They didn't look like dockhands. They looked like soldiers who had put on the wrong clothes.

Cassie exhaled once, slow. "Now."

The floodlights snapped on. White glare poured down the lane.

Shouts. Weapons raised.

The first shot cracked the night open. Cassie dropped into a crouch as the sound tore past her ear. LAPD fired back, muzzle flashes strobing against steel walls. Bullets sparked off metal.

She ducked behind the fender of a forklift, heart hammering. Gravel spat near her boot. She leaned out, sighted, squeezed, and one of the men staggered and fell back against the container, red blooming across his shirt.

Skael barked something, could've been a command or a curse. He fired wild down the lane. One of Cassie's detectives spun, hit in the shoulder, dragging himself behind cover with a scream that sounded too human for this kind of night.

Cassie pushed forward. Keep pressure. Don't let them reset.

The truck's engine roared. "Michael, Christ, it's Michael," she thought as she saw Kareth stumble from behind the wheel, blood already wetting his side, firing one-handed toward the lights. He clipped a lamp. Sparks showered down like angry fireflies.

Cassie pressed into the chaos, every nerve screaming, until she was ten meters from the container. Skael was there, closing the distance, weapon leveled. His eyes caught hers, sharp even in the glare.

She fired first.

The impact threw him sideways. His gun clattered across the concrete.

Silence didn't come immediately; it arrived in ragged pieces, broken by the groan of one man, a cough from another, the last spin of a bullet casing clinking against steel.

Cassie rose, chest heaving, the taste of copper in her mouth, though it wasn't her blood. She scanned—four of them down, Lionel included. Michael was gone, vanished into the dark with the sound of a coughing engine.

The LAPD detective clutched his shoulder, pale but alive. Marsten crouched beside him, pressing a cloth hard against the wound.

Cassie stood in the wreckage of lane twelve, gun still warm in her grip, floodlights hissing overhead.

Another night, another pile of bodies that weren't supposed to exist.

She was still catching her breath, the echoes of the raid ringing in her ears, when her phone vibrated. She answered, still scanning the scene.

David didn't waste time with pleasantries.

"Cassie," his voice was clipped, urgent. "The boss wants to speak with you. Now."

She froze. "The boss?"

"*The* boss," David confirmed. No mistaking who he meant.

The closest craft woke, not with drama, no theatrical fog or movie sound, but with a composure that felt like confidence turned into movement. A seal unsealed. Air exhaled like memory leaving a room. The hatch slid, not on rails, but on a decision.

A humanoid figure moved within and stepped forward. The suit was matte, not glossy; the helmet a dark mirror with no hint of a face beneath. There was grace; there was readiness. It spoke, and the sound was the sound of a language that would have made no sense two years ago and made absolute sense to Jude now.

"Takra Vael," the figure said. The consonants folded into Jude's head as if the skull had been carved to fit them. "We bring respect. We bring reports. I am Revra of the Second Regiment."

"Name and station," Vael said inside Jude, reflex bringing rank forward like a weapon.

Jude's mouth didn't move. His hearing did. The part of him that answered people did not belong entirely to him anymore.

The helmet turned. It registered the congresswoman's presence as a thing to log, not a thing to negotiate. "The honorable Nireva," the figure said in English—or rather, the Aethero tongue had started to sound like English to Jude's ears.

It looked back at Jude. Jude heard the words that were not words. "The journey was perilous. We cut many cycles across chokeholds," the figure said. "Assembly teeth everywhere. We were not bitten. Our trail is cold."

"That will change," Jude said, in his own voice. "Everything changes faster than you plan."

The helmet inclined. "We planned for that too."

Nireva hated ritual when it wasn't hers. "Where are our serums?" she asked. "I want to jab myself and be able to set foot again in Aethrie, even if in this body."

"Here," the figure said, and a panel on the side of the craft's skin peeled back as if the wall had always been a wardrobe. Within, harnesses hung like siding made for men who had been measured a long time ago, and a metal case containing inoculations. The engineer took a half-step he didn't mean to take.

Jude didn't move toward the suits. He looked at Rakkar. "Inside," he said, low. "Give me the last two years. Routes, stops, transmissions, changes of doctrine. And give me the world on the way; traffic, anomalous emissions, the places they didn't go that tell you more than the places they did."

Rakkar nodded. He slung the laptop and the hardline kit and followed the figure's gesture up a small set of composite stairs into the open hatch. He didn't hesitate. Rakkar believed in numbers the way certain people believed in confession.

Chapter 19: RECONNAISSANCE

The hangar was not supposed to exist. Concrete poured without permits, electricity drawn from phantom grids, its presence erased from every register that mattered. Yet here it was, sunk into Nebraska earth, and inside it the craft rested like a black seed grown in the wrong soil.

The air smelled of warm metal and something older, a tang that did not belong to this planet, though it was here now. The resonance carried through the walls, through the ribcage. Not noise, not quite. A pressure that made breathing a measured act.

Hansen hovered, unsure of his role now that the future had walked into his warehouse. “I can get more people,” he offered. “If you want more hands on, not on them, I mean, on the systems.”

“Fewer people means fewer reports written badly,” Jude said. “Hold your team outside the perimeter.”

“Right,” Hansen said, chest falling as if reminded he was breathing.

Jude felt Nireva step inside before he looked. Her hair was tied back sharp, the gesture that always traded ornament for control. She held her phone face down in her palm like a dealer deciding when the table deserved to see a card.

“Your escorts aren’t answering,” she said. No ornament in her voice either.

“They’re busy, I assume. Big cargo,” Jude said. “Yours?”

"Mine are quiet too," she replied. Her eyes didn't shift. "Too quiet. When men with ambition fall silent, it is never because nothing is happening."

Jude let the line hang long enough for it to sound like agreement, long enough for her to wonder.

"I'll make another call. Locals always hear what professionals think they've buried," she said at last, already half-turned.

He watched her leave, the silence following her out like another operative.

Rakkar led him forward. Boots on alloy. The space hummed around them, the soundless vibration of systems that had never been built by human hands, though they now sat on human ground.

"Thirty minutes of broadcast," Rakkar said. His voice was even, no flourish, no surprise. "It loops. Always the same."

Jude looked at the vessel, its surface the color of void, its angles wrong in the light. He felt the breath he took adjust itself to the rhythm of the hum. He nodded once.

"Let's hear it."

The sound began. Not as voice, not at first. As vibration. The floor seemed to carry it upward into bone, chest, jaw. It pressed into the body before it reached the ear. A pulse. A rhythm. Regular, unrelenting.

Then it shifted. Cadence. Intonation. A pattern unmistakable to anything that had ever heard language. The distortion resolved until words began to surface, vowels drawn long, consonants bent.

"Divine engines bore us through silence. The steel bent but did not break. We walked between stars, and the dark did not take us. We remain."

The words repeated, slightly altered each time. The rhythm did not vary, but the accents slid, pulling each phrase in and out of focus.

Rakkar's eyes were half-closed, listening as one who already knew. Jude stood very still. His chest tightened. His breath had fallen into the chant without permission.

Another verse rose, heavier:

"Bound by covenant. Carried by oath. Our fathers swore upon the light and were not broken. We remain."

The air thickened with it. Lights in the hangar flickered as though they too were caught in its cadence. Jude felt the walls pulse. Felt the marrow of his own bones align.

He said nothing.

The liturgy carried on:

"We are the Children of Aethrie. We are not lost. We remember."

The vowels scraped. They were wrong enough to feel alien, right enough to strike memory. Jude felt something tighten at the base of his skull, as if the words were chiseling at a memory he did not have.

Rakkar opened his eyes. He did not smile. He only said, "Scripture. Memory performed until it becomes law. This is how they live, how we used to live."

Jude let the next verse pass before speaking. His voice was low. "Anything on Earth?"

Rakkar looked at him. "That is the part I didn't believe. Until now."

From the corner of the chamber, movement. Revra. Black armor, visor opaque, steps measured. Not film, not recording—present, here, the air shifting with the weight of its tread.

The chant carried on, undisturbed.

Revra's hands rose. Fingers touched the latch at the side of the helmet. A sharp metallic click echoed, too loud against the surrounding silence. A hiss escaped, white and thin, as if the suit itself exhaled.

Condensation bloomed across the inside of the visor, fogging it opaque. For a moment, it was only a mirror, reflecting Jude back at himself—bent, curved, face stretched, fractured. The reflection split as the visor began to lift.

Slowly. Not ceremony, not theatre. Deliberation. Each degree of motion carried weight. The hiss lingered, steam bleeding into the air between them.

The visor came away.

A face. Skin pale from the absence of light. Jaw was roughened by hair not perfectly cut, by a razor that had missed. A mole beneath the left eye. A mark that might have been a childhood scar. Lines of faded blue moved like rivers charted across skin: not paint, not decoration, but an inheritance lying under hairline and jawline like a map that had become flesh. Yet this was nothing mythic. Nothing foreign. Ordinary enough to collapse the distance between worlds. There was no doubt—the face was *human*.

"*We remain.*" The chant did not falter. "*We return,*" it added. The words pressed closer now, no longer distant scripture but proof in flesh. Each syllable struck against the face before them, confirmation with every beat.

Rakkar stared, not at the humanity of it—that he already knew—but at the resonance between the chant and the soil under their feet. His voice came low, as if speaking risked shattering the weight of it.

"This world," he said, "is not one we found. It is the one we left. *Earth is Old Aethrie.*"

The words settled in the chamber like stone dropped into water.

Jude did not move. His eyes stayed on the face. His body was still, but his pulse pounded. Inside the white expanse, Vael gave nothing. Not rage, not denial, not command. Only silence, heavy enough to be confirmation.

The chanting went on. "*We remain. We return.*"

Jude felt his own breath catch against the words. The thought was already there. It did not need volume. It was written in the silence that followed Rakkar's confession, in the human face before him, in the pulse that would not stop.

They were us. They *are* us.

Jude stayed where he was because moving would have made something break. He felt his phone buzz again and did not take it out.

He thought of a woman in Whitehall flying across oceans to be by his side. He thought of men and women on Terminal Island trying to decide, and deciding too late, whether to shoot first. He thought of a London kitchen where a sister purposefully turned away from a kettle that had not boiled, telling herself she would not cry because that would be conceding things she did not want to concede.

He thought of the word *Earth* and how it sounded different when the people saying it were not his prior definition of human.

Back in Washington, Ella closed a door quietly behind a woman from Commerce, who had just told her a story about port tariffs and had not realized she was confessing to a different kind of traffic. Ella wrote two names in her notebook that looked like budget codes, but were not.

The corridor was quiet enough to hear shoes argue with the carpet. She waited until the woman's footsteps merged into someone else's camera feed, then slipped out through a side exit that did not badge properly. She could have gone home. She did not.

At a bar that prided itself on being unfashionable, she listened to the room the way one listens to static for a signal. A man at the counter was explaining how drones had changed the nature of surveillance. Another voice carried three words that mattered more than the rest: *Graves, Jude, Nebraska.* He wasn't speaking to her. He wasn't even careful.

Ella let her drink warm, untouched. She thought about Jennifer Graves, the neatness of her votes, the whispers that her office reached farther than it should. She thought about Jude, the way his name kept bleeding through systems that had no reason to touch each other. And now Nebraska, showing up not as agriculture, not as defense, but in procurement flows tucked under health and transport, like someone trying too hard to look boring.

She left a tip she did not owe, walked outside, and called no one. Instead, she sat on a bench where the streetlamps made a lattice of light and shadow and scrolled a news brief she was not meant to see: CIA, NSA, DIA, suddenly talking to each other in a way that meant something had spooked them. MI5 and MI6 were copied on the memos. MoD watching quietly from across the ocean. A word repeated twice in the chatter: Papillion.

Ella stared at it until the word felt like a decision. She booked a flight to Omaha with her thumb before her body had decided to stand. Sometimes choices feel inevitable only after one has already made them.

Cassie was ferried through two layers of gates and three layers of questions before anyone told her where she was. Offutt Air Force Base spread flat against the Nebraska dark, low buildings lit with the dull glow of a place that never stopped humming.

She had been here once before, years ago, for a liaison exercise she wasn't senior enough to remember. Tonight, the air smelled of jet fuel and damp concrete, and the men checking her badge looked like they had stopped bothering to pretend they were only soldiers.

Inside, they took her phone, her gun, and the sense of being ordinary. A guard walked her down a corridor of polished linoleum that reflected light too clean to be comforting. The last door opened into a room with no windows and a table that already knew the weight of classified conversations.

The man waiting there didn't stand. He didn't need to. White hair. Sharp suit. The stillness of someone who knew half the world's secrets and had stopped being impressed by them decades ago. Cassie didn't need the introduction.

"Director," she said, because calling him anything else would have been a lie.

"Sit," he said. His voice was even, clipped, the kind used to being obeyed before the second syllable.

She sat.

"We've been watching you," he began. "Not in the way you might think. We didn't plant bugs in your walls. We let you run because we needed someone stubborn enough to see patterns when everyone else filed them away." He slid a folder across the table, its cover marked with an innocuous code number that meant everything to those who used it.

She didn't open it. "Patterns like Hampshire."

His mouth twitched once, never a smile. "Good. You're already on the right page. Hampshire was the first. A pod. Not debris. Not foreign tech. Alien."

Cassie's eyes widened. She leaned forward, palms flat on the desk.

"When our squad touched it, the first man—Sergeant Wallace," The name landed like a weight. "He changed. Not visibly, not at once. But something moved inside him. We called it possession. Others in the room said assimilation. His family was informed he died in the line of duty. Truthfully, he lived in a basement we never marked on a map for twelve months more. Long enough for us to pull every word he had in him. We didn't like what we heard."

Cassie's fingers stayed flat on the table. "And you buried it."

"We contained it," the Director corrected. "Same way we contained everything else since. Shanghai. Paris. New York. We've known for two years that these aren't isolated incidents. Small dark objects have crash-landed. Teams have formed around them. Some wear government names. Some wear private ones. None are what they say they are. Black. Lin. Graves. You've chased them. We've monitored them."

"Why not step in?"

He leaned forward a fraction, the closest he came to emphasis. "Because this is bigger than one raid in one city. We saw early what it took you months to prove: they're not just building networks. They're preparing for something. And if we moved too soon, we'd lose our chance to see the scale."

The room held its own silence for a moment.

Cassie found her voice steady. "And now?"

He opened the folder. Satellite photos, raw and grainy, lay inside: heat blooms against dark soil, streaks of descent. "Two nights ago, we caught a signal. Cadence doesn't match any terrestrial broadcast. It came just before three signatures landed in Nebraska."

She looked up. "Recon ships."

"That's our assessment," he said. "Three crafts. Their size, their design—nothing human. But the moment they landed, the satellites we had trained on the area went blind. Cut. Like someone reached up and closed their fists around our eyes. Since then: nothing."

Cassie exhaled slowly. The thought came out before she could stop it. "You fear the worst."

"We always do," the Director said. "But this time we might be right."

Cassie sat back, letting the words burn. Two years of chasing shadows across ports, alleyways, and safehouses in half-dead cities: Paris, Shanghai, Los Angeles. Two years of Jude slipping ahead, always half a step, always leaving just enough trace to make her follow. She had called it cat and mouse. But it had been cartography all along, her drawing the outline of something vaster. Every inexplicable shipment, every flare of violence that didn't belong, every alias in the wrong manifest, it all fit now, like stars in a map you didn't know you were reading until someone drew the lines.

She thought of Wallace, the soldier whose life had been chewed down to nothing but words in a basement. She thought of the face Jude wore when he told her truths that had to be lies, and lies that had to be truths. She felt the ground tilt for the first time, not because of him, but because the world itself had shifted.

“Why me?” she asked at last. Her voice was quieter than she meant. “You have analysts. You have satellites. You have every tool in the world. Why am I sitting here?”

The Director closed the folder with a sound of finality. “Because you’re already inside it. Black is an outlier, and he chose you as his mirror. That makes you the one thing they don’t plan for: a variable they can’t erase. Which means now you belong to the bigger picture, whether you wanted it or not.”

Cassie held his gaze, even as the weight of the room pressed against her shoulders. Somewhere, in the silence that followed, she understood: the chase was over. The war had begun.

Chapter 20:
INERTIA

Two days later

The hangar had learned the shape of them.

It knew the cadence of Jude's footsteps and how he slowed before the central plinth where the recon craft fed their minds back into themselves. It knew the sound of Rakkar's keys; the quick, clean bursts of code that never needed to be loud to be precise. It knew Revra's weight; armor quiet, voice quiet, authority obvious only in the way others arranged themselves around him without realizing it. And it knew Nireva by temperature shift alone: rooms went brighter when she entered, not because the bulbs changed but because attention did.

Jude stood at the Aethero console as if it were an instrument he'd practiced on in a childhood he hadn't had. Vael had fought him at first—not like this, not that switch, not that cascade—but Revra had stepped in with a soldier's patience and a priest's care. "You cannot break what you understand," he had said. "You will understand faster if it answers you." Rakkar had watched, eyes narrowing in the particular way they did when a puzzle admitted it had edges.

The interface wasn't screens and menus; it was a field, tangible and not. A slab of composite that accepted hand pressure like a question: slide here, and star maps unfolded in glowing ridges; press there, and the weapons manifest rose like a warning. Jude had learned where to push to peel back the last two years: Aethrie's arc through Assembly patrol corridors; safe lanes plotted and replotted; moments when the worldship's engines throttled down to the sound of a held breath. He had learned to open the weapons inventory and then shut it again before Vael could press the hunger into him, finding his own reflection in the dead panel for a second. Alien glass made him look older.

The weapons were there, wrapped in understatement. Two pallets of shaped ordnance that weren't just bombs; they were lessons in how gravity could be made to obey a blade. Micro-lances for hull cutting. Shock-matter charges for doors that thought they were unopenable. His throat tightened as he lingered on the schematics. He closed the manifest before Vael could press the hunger into him.

Revra stood to his left, visor up, the blue traceries along his jaw stark in the hangar light. "You have hands like a pilot," he said, not flattery, but observation.

"Pilots break too, if they lean on instruments they don't understand," Jude said, letting the route map bleed away under his palm. "I've seen it."

Nireva arrived on a gust of controlled air. "Status?"

"It shows what we already know," Rakkar replied. "Five inoculated. Sixth prepped when we have substrate ready. Four recon crew resting, one in quarantine. Revra active. Your engineer, Hansen, has the local systems where you wanted them: oxygen, heat, and feed lines. I've crawled most of their logs. We know where they throttled to dark. We know where they didn't."

"We also know you've been moving things we did not authorize," Vael murmured from the cage in Jude's head.

Jude ignored him and brushed the console to a different perspective: the quiet funnel where the recon boats had dropped down through blind sky.

"We stayed invisible. We didn't get bit," said Revra.

"Until they landed," Rakkar added softly, from a workstation he'd claimed and rebuilt until it looked like an argument he was winning. "Satellites disabled. The sky went blind."

"Sooner or later, that trick gets noticed," Jude said.

Rakkar slid a display toward him and Nireva. "Domestic production," he said. "Nebraska's throughput is higher than Hansen admitted to you in the first tour, and lower than he told Procurement." A ghost of amusement touched his mouth. "He's honest by accident."

"Numbers," Nireva said.

"Two lines active. One staged. A million vials per line per week at current cycle times if the cold chain holds. They're ready to package one block." He didn't look away from the data. "We just need the cargo from Los Angeles to arrive."

Nireva's nails clicked once on the table, the only sign she'd heard. "Five million on hand," she said, not as a question, but as if testing the weight of the number aloud.

"Five million," Rakkar confirmed.

She didn't let herself breathe while her mind did the math. Five million bodies made viable for foreign air meant five million who could land first and hold doors for five more. It wasn't a victory. It was momentum. Sometimes momentum was more useful.

"But where is the delivery?" Her voice cracked, sharp enough that even Hansen, a few feet away, tilted his head.

Cassie stared at the warehouse wall until the cinderblocks went back to being just concrete. Walls are just walls until someone hides something inside them.

The task force had taken a slice of Offutt and staged it as an office; in truth, it was a room with two clocks, twenty screens, and a smell like recycled conversations.

"Say it again," the Air Force colonel said, as if repetition might make the number smaller.

"Five million vials worth," Cassie answered, recalling the report that came out after the port raid. She put her finger on the still, grainy image of Nebraska from an hour ago. "If that's the first batch, we have the privilege of being early to the party. If it's the last..."

"It isn't," David said from the corner, his voice soft with fatigue and certainty. "It never is."

A DHS woman who looked as if she'd been born with a badge clipped to her lanyard scrubbed her face. "We can't just bomb it," she said, the weariness in her tone betraying the committees that would crucify her for the suggestion.

"No," the colonel said dryly. "Because it isn't only a lab."

Cassie turned that over. He was right, and she knew it. You didn't stack that much cold-chain next to that much hardened concrete unless you were pretending to have one job while outfitting another. Arms. Storage. An inventory that made a building double as both throat and fist.

"We do both," Cassie said. "Visible and invisible. You give them a show at the fence so they think you're the whole story. Meanwhile, I put people inside who know what to do when a room pretends it's just a room."

The colonel looked at her the way career officers look at civilians when the civilians are inconveniently correct. "Timing?"

"This week," she said. "Before the next shipment arrives via another route." She didn't add, and before whoever's running this burns the place to save the secret. The room didn't need it said aloud.

Someone asked gently, because it mattered, "Do you have a line to Black?"

"No," Cassie said. "He calls me when he wants me in position. He doesn't answer when I want him anywhere." She swallowed a mix of pride and exhausted fury. "We move on what we can prove, not on insiders who live in our heads."

She went back to the pictures and drew a map you couldn't pull from any satellite: the gate that stuck if you lifted before you pushed; the blind strip between two cameras that overlapped everywhere except one lazy inch; the utility corridor that never aerated properly, where sound carried like gossip in a church hall.

"Distraction here," she said. "Entry there. Extraction through here when it goes loud."

David watched quietly and thought, not for the first time, that she looked most like herself when the world demanded the impossible and she wrote down the possible anyway.

Around the table, some of the patriots weren't even listening to her map; they were caught instead in the history they thought they were about to make. The first armed clash on American soil in living memory. The kind of milestone men mistook for glory before it ever arrived.

The silence in Nireva's office at the lab wasn't quiet; it was a withheld explosion. She had been at her desk for an hour and had not once looked at the country scenery. The fewer grand things she saw, the sharper her mind became. Sharp was the only shape she trusted herself in.

Her phone lay face-up and treacherous. No pings from the people who usually didn't fail to ping: the senator who enjoyed being first to tell her which way his security committee would lean, the minority member louder in texts than in hearings. Silence from both.

The Los Angeles report blazed on the screen at the page that mattered: four bodies she had sent; none returning. Lionel Smith, the name of Skael's host on the list, made something twist in her chest she refused to honor with grief. She'd liked him. She liked all machines that never once pretended to be men.

"Too neat," she said to the empty room. "Too fast. No move that clean wasn't rehearsed."

She called Viktor, the Russian leading her small army of mercenaries stationed at the facility. He answered on the second ring. "Did you want an update? We're inside cycle three. Everything holds. You want me to..."

"I want you to stop trying to reassure me," she said. "Lock the west gate. Tighten personnel lists. If any truck comes without three separate pretexts, it doesn't arrive. Do not burn anything unless I tell you to. Do you understand that order?"

"Yes," he said, after a brief pause.

She hung up before he could say *ma'am*. She didn't like being anyone's ma'am when the ground was moving.

Her screen pulsed with another small insult: her staffer's note that tomorrow's security committee pre-brief had been rescheduled. The kind of rescheduling that meant someone who mattered wanted to be somewhere else on time.

She felt the shape of a small mole and hated that the thought tasted too much like vanity. If it was a leak, it was because she had been good enough to matter. If it were simply competence on the other side, she would not flatter them by calling it betrayal.

She closed the laptop and stood very still until stillness stopped being the same thing as waiting.

Ella parked her rental a hundred meters from the warehouse perimeter, headlights off, engine ticking in the dark. The compound looked inert—fence, sodium lamps buzzing overhead, flat concrete buildings that wore their disguise too well. But she'd been in enough cities, enough meetings, enough bad rooms in Whitehall to know when something hummed beneath the surface. This place hummed.

She lifted her burner, typed Jude's name into a message field, stared at it, then erased the words. Tried again. I'm here. Deleted that too. She pressed send on nothing. The screen stayed blank, indifferent.

A scrape of gravel drew her eyes to the side mirror. Three men in security jackets emerged from the shadows where she hadn't seen a door, rifles slung casually. Their faces weren't bored like rent-a-cops. They were alert. They already knew.

One rapped his knuckles against her window. The glass shook.

“Out,” he said. “Now.”

Ella’s heartbeat kicked once hard against her ribs. She slid the burner low, tucked it into the thin pocket under the driver’s seat, fingers moving like she’d done it a thousand times. Then she opened the door.

The nearest man stepped back, gesturing toward the compound. “Follow.”

She did. Not because she trusted them, but because running into a Nebraska night with three rifles at her back was suicide. She memorized their strides, the way the taller one favored his left knee, the second’s jacket bulged at the hip with more than one weapon. She’d need those details later, if later came.

“Movements,” Rakkar said moments later, his voice betraying nothing of the speed at which he processed. “Air Force. Clean arcs. Quiet comms. They flew this pattern over Iraq and called it prudence. They’re tightening.” His words carried the weight of hours studying human military formations.

Jude had been standing so still that the console had begun to mirror him. The room shifted around Rakkar’s words. His body moved on its own: breath out, shoulders set, mind reaching for the board he wasn’t supposed to touch alone.

Viktor’s voice cracked over the internal line. “Intruder on the perimeter. Female. We’ve detained her. What do you want done?”

“Her?” Jude said before he could stop himself.

Through the glass, he saw her, and the second he did, he understood that all the timing he’d built was now wrong. Ella didn’t belong here. She belonged anywhere else. So here she was.

Vael’s palm flattened against the bars. *“She is the seam. Every wall splits at the seam.”*

Rakkar didn't look away from his screen. "If we wait any longer, we'll be fighting the wrong fight at the wrong gate. Whatever we do, we do it now." With Jude's consent, he went with Revra to call up the rest of the recon crew.

Jude closed his eyes and saw the map of corridors he'd laid out in his head for a different day. He opened them and saw Ella, jaw set, walking into a bad room she already understood. Between those two images lay a line he'd drawn without admitting it.

He pressed his hands to the Aethero field. It woke under his palms, subtle enough to pique Vael's interest.

Jude called up datasets the recon ships had used to whisper past Assembly teeth. He inverted it, spread the band instead of narrowing it, pouring a pattern through the Nebraska air that would look like a wounded signal to anyone familiar with the old cadences, and like nothing to anyone who wasn't. A flare that wasn't a flare. A confession wrapped as distress. A map only the right enemies could read.

"Don't," Vael said, too late for an order, exactly in time for a curse.

Jude let the network climb, hook into the atmosphere, find friends hidden beyond sight. Somewhere past the solar system, to the nearest Assembly checkpoint.

He didn't stop. He peeled off a copy of the lab's internals, a map with the lies removed, and broke it into pieces small enough to travel along the channels he knew Cassie would watch, even when she told herself she wasn't. Door codes for the inner ring. The west gate that locked dirty unless lifted before pushing. The blind inch between cameras. Places where a wrong bullet would trigger a right bomb.

He routed the pieces through three servers, down a pipe a municipal contractor had left open. He added a line: Don't kick the west wall unless you want to leave in pieces. No signature. No need.

He switched screens and turned to see the Aethero crew approaching, flanked by Nireva and Rakkar, all suited for battle.

Jude went into the other room, where Ella was held by two men, standing across the glass and watching him. She didn't know what he'd done, but she felt it, the shift in the room that changed the air before explanation. Jude looked at her with quiet steadiness, lifted his hand, palm out, not quite a wave. She didn't mirror it. She only tilted her chin the way she used to when she decided in advance to forgive him for things he hadn't yet done.

"Found her in a car, sir," one of the mercenaries said, breath tight with adrenaline and borrowed victory. "No badge. Scoped the yard like it owed her something."

Jude didn't have time to respond.

No alarms rang. That wasn't how nights like this worked. Instead, signals moved quietly. Somewhere above Omaha, a flight path bent. Farther out, a listening post caught the echo of a pattern it shouldn't have heard and snapped awake. And farther still, in the dark beyond planets, a quiet ping tethered itself to silence that hadn't been broken in years."

Jude's palms tingled as if the field had bitten him. He had acted earlier than he'd planned. He had pulled a door open that would not close without cost. He looked once at Ella through the glass, once at the recon ships waiting like loaded rooms, once at Nireva through the door—because Nireva would be the first to understand what they had just attracted into their territory.

"Positions!" Jude growled. It wasn't for his sake. It was so that the men who had trusted him wouldn't die foolishly.

Rakkar was already at his station, fingers quick. Revra pulled his visor down. Nireva moved next to Jude, determined but still unsure who to trust. And on a screen in an operations room, Cassie's feed blinked, then filled with a map that shouldn't exist—codes, blind spots, entry points Jude had pushed into her hands.

Jude stood still and felt the weight of it sink into him. Vael's voice slammed against the inside of his skull. *"You fool. You've lit the sky too soon. You think you command the storm, but you've only told it where to strike."*

Jude clenched his jaw, not answering at first. He felt Ella's eyes on him through the glass, steady and unflinching.

"It's the right time," he said finally, quiet enough that it could have been meant only for himself.

Chapter 21:
COLLISION

The prairie had learned the weight of tractors, not armor.

Out beyond the ring of cottonwoods and irrigation pivots, a line of headlights unspooled across the dark-like beads on a wire. Engines growled, brakes hissed, and wind pushed dust into low ghosts that hung over the fields and refused to disperse. Overhead, drones wrote silent circles into the night, their sensors peeling heat from shadow. The smell was fuel, damp soil, and the metallic tang of rain that couldn't quite commit.

Inside the complex, poured concrete and steel ribs pretending to be agriculture, the air hummed with a deeper frequency. The recon craft in Bay One vibrated in the bones, a soundless pressure that insisted on attention. Technicians who thought they were engineers clung to clipboards because clipboards were how people pretended order would outlast chaos.

Rakkar stood over the central console, face lit by bad software and good data. "They've split their approach," he said. "Armor down County Road 370, dismounts through the north drainage, helos staging over the river. Whoever stacked this plan read us like we were a diagram."

"They're guessing the shape," Jude said. He didn't look at the screen; he looked at the doors. "Tonight we match it."

Across the floor, Nireva watched the perimeter feeds as if she could will the image to behave. She carried her control like a blade and didn't bother to sheath it. "Hold them at the outer fence," she told a mercenary at her shoulder. "Keep the east service road clear. If the line breaks there, we're blind."

"It won't," the man said. It would, but men like him were paid to believe their mouths.

Revra rolled his shoulders under the battle suit, and the suit answered by sealing a rib of dark alloy over his collarbone with a soft clack. Five more figures mirrored the motion: six shadows in matte plating that drank the light and showed nothing back. Their visors were mirror-dark; their gauntlets flexed as though they were alive.

"Shield matrix on my mark," Revra said in the Aethero tongue, the words a rhythm that would have sounded alien to anyone else and to Jude sounded like orders; clean, old, cut to fit a soldier's mouth. "Cut lines at range. No trophies. No captures. We leave no angles for them to learn."

"Yes," came the chorus, quiet and precise.

Nireva tracked them with a glance, that tiny, betraying lift of the chin she reserved for things she admired and pretended not to. "Try not to die," she said dry. "It's a poor use of resources."

Revra didn't waste words on a woman with no command over him. He palmed the bay door release. Cold air shoved through the gap as the panel rose, dragging prairie scent into the hangar and washing the recycled air from the room. A wind like fingers went along everyone's skin. The first tracer rounds stitched red lines across the opening. Revra stepped into them and kept going.

The six recon suits fanned into the yard, their footfalls too light for the bulk they carried. From the berm at the far edge, an Abrams tank ground into view, its treads chewing dirt, its turret already seeking a target. Revra raised his gauntlet. A beam cut from his palm; thin, white, merciless. It looked like a searchlight until it touched steel. The Abrams shuddered. Its turret jerked as if struck by an invisible fist. The main barrel drooped, glowing red at the seam, before tearing down the middle. Armor across the glacis plate unzipped under the beam, peeling in long molten strips that curled like paper in a fire. The sound followed an instant later: the shriek of riven metal, then a concussion that slapped the hangar doors hard enough to rattle the bolts.

Cassie moved with her team along the blind strip between cameras, the concrete sweating from the concussion outside. She had asked for a distraction. She hadn't asked for the earth to sound like it was tearing in half.

The utility corridor was dark, with only thin slits of light where vents leaked through. She caught one of those slits and froze. Out in the yard, the six recon suits fanned, black metal moving with too much grace for their bulk. They didn't look like men in armor. They looked like weapons that had decided to walk.

In Syria, villages cracked open under artillery, and men in cheap body armor thought they were tanks because they shouted loud enough. She'd watched an airstrike turn a block into dust and fire and still leave someone alive enough to scream. None of it looked like this.

One of the suits lifted its gauntlet, and a tank folded in half. The light didn't flash, it cut. The turret sagged as if it were paper, steel peeling down the glacis like wet cardboard. Cassie's mouth went dry.

Her people stared too long. She hissed, "Eyes forward," because if they froze here, they were already dead.

Cassie felt the calculus crawl cold through her head. Six suits were enough to stall a combined-arms strike. Six. And in L.A., they busted five million vials.

Five million of them on Earth.

The thought made her stomach flip. Whole armies would look like police barricades. Cities would last hours, not days.

She forced her eyes back to the corridor. The utility door was ahead. Her team's boots scraped concrete, too loud, every sound a betrayal. She kept her weapon close and her fear closer.

"This way," she whispered. Not because she believed it would work. But because the alternative was stopping to watch gods walk, and she had seen enough already to know what happened to people who stopped.

Infantry broke from cover along the fenceline. Their muzzle flashes strobed. The recon suits moved in straight lines like geometry was a weapon. Energy darts stitched through torsos and left nothing but exhaustion in their wake. A rocket drew its lazy spiral toward the hangar mouth. Two suits swung together, and a hexagonal panel unfurled between them with a sound like a swarm. The rocket hit and shaved the edge off the light. Fracture lines spread through the pattern like frost.

"Beautiful," Rakkar said under his breath, and the word sounded like a sin to him.

"Expensive," Nireva said.

"Temporary," Jude said.

The shield matrix held another two strikes and then blew apart into sparks that looked like a million starlings taking flight. The recon suits didn't wait for the next salvo; they moved. One launched into the air with a controlled kick, boosters hissing a minimal protest, and landed on the engine deck of an MRAP with the surety of a dancer stepping onto a mark. A blade of light—no thicker than a hand, all edge—anchored, drew, and the roof peeled back. The men inside didn't even have time to scream.

Helicopters scissored the air. Flares fell. The sky turned into a carnival of wrong colors. The recon suits cut two of the birds out of the air, one by shearing a tail boom, one by throwing an energy lance through the cockpit like a rail driven into soft ground, and still there were three more. Numbers write their own doctrine.

Jude leaned over the railing and watched the battle take its shape—columns advancing, arcs closing, doctrine unfolding like it had been written into the ground long before either side arrived. The threat of a full-scale Aethero invasion now etched in his mind.

"You enjoy this," Nireva said. It wasn't a question.

"I like honesty," Jude replied. "Combat makes liars shut up. You see only what works and what breaks."

"Honesty is wasteful," she said. "Uncertainty keeps people alive. Ambiguity keeps doors open. Clarity just writes names for headstones."

"Then you should have planned for headstones," Jude said, channeling his inner Vael. He said it softly, almost kindly, and that was what made it cruel.

In fact, at that moment, all he cared about was that his plan to escape—with Ella—was in motion.

On the floor below, mercenaries used crates as cover, their rifles cracking in the layered way of men with training that had never been tested this hard. They were brave, and bravery is useful until it isn't. One woman dragged another behind a forklift and put her hand over the other's throat, where something red spurted and failed to slow. A man ducked, stood, and didn't duck fast enough. Their courage had no language that belonged to this fight.

"East service road," Rakkar said, switching cameras. "They brought a breaching team. Thermite on the gate pins in three, two..."

The feed flared white as the gate gave. A wedge of men appeared in the resulting smoke, no insignia visible, motion all business. A small tracked robot zipped through the gap, turned a camera eye like a curious animal, and spat a grenade with the indifference of a device. The blast took the corner off the loading bay.

"Push them back," Nireva snapped into a radio that pretended this was still the old kind of battle. "Now."

"They're not yours to push anymore," Rakkar said softly.

She pretended not to hear.

Revra cut a path across the yard and barked for a pullback—suits collected, regrouped, shield matrix for the next two seconds—when something new entered the air. A keening, low at first, then climbing until it found the frequency where human bodies start to hate sound.

"EW?" Rakkar asked.

"Maybe," Jude said, because the answer didn't matter. You don't out-argue a drone. You turn its story into yours or get written out of it.

The high-pitched noise of incoming rockets shifted into a brutal pressure wave. The recon suits staggered, their silhouettes jolting out of rhythm for a single, vulnerable heartbeat. Overhead, the helicopter banked and fired again. The impact lit the yard—white, then yellow, then the raw glare of pain itself.

When the smoke peeled back, two of the suits were down on one knee, armor scorched and plates buckled. Revra planted himself between them, gauntlets raised, body angled to take the next strike. The others tightened into a wedge, shields overlapping, bracing against the assault.

The suits weren't flawless, but they had been built for this. Older than the word "drone," forged for wars before humans had named the sky, they still knew exactly what to do when the heavens decided to kill you.

"Enough," Rakkar said. He didn't raise his voice; he didn't need to. He was not making a suggestion. He was handing out physics. "We scuttle."

Nireva tore her gaze from the yard and gave him a look that would have counted as lethal if it could be metabolized. "You set charges in my lab without permission," she said. She meant my dominion.

"I set charges on our vulnerabilities," Rakkar said, his loyalty not revealing the fact that he had followed Jude's instructions. He let the word hang. It was the one thing they all still recognized as sacred.

Jude put a hand on Rakkar's shoulder, only long enough to be read as assent.

"We burn it," he said. "All of it. We can't afford humans getting their hands on our weaponry, so early in this war."

Nireva smiled, small and thin, the way a woman smiles at the moment she commits to hating you permanently. "You always were better at torching than tending." The tone had a personal tinge.

"Ends are a kind of tending," Jude said.

He turned away before the sentence could curdle into something else.

"Arm the grid," Rakkar said into his mic. "White channels only. Staggered delay. If you see me run, you're late."

The hangar lights flickered as the charges woke on lines no one but Rakkar had ever drawn. In the maintenance corridors, small LEDs blinked the message only men who were afraid of the dark learn to love: soon.

From the side door, two mercenaries half-dragged, half-walked Ella into the open, her arms bound behind her back with the kind of zip-tie that bites and keeps biting

Jude didn't have to see her face. The way she held her head was enough.

"Leave her here," he said, and they obliged. His voice didn't change. He had learned the trick. It still costs him.

"Your taste in complications," Nireva said, "remains expensive."

"I have use for her," Jude shot back, and the awkwardness felt like the first time someone uses your true name in a room full of strangers.

Ella turned once and met Jude's eyes. He didn't shake his head; shaking is information. He just looked at her the way a man looks at a door he already knows he has to go through.

The US wedge brought up a second wave on the feeds, shields angled, mechanics clean. Whoever held the board on the other side had done this before. They were not improvising. They were executing.

"Air's thickening," Rakkar said. "We've got thirty minutes max before they own the perimeter."

"We arm in twenty," Jude said. He didn't look at the clock. He looked at Bay One, where the recon craft waited, hatch open like an outstretched hand.

Revra cut back in hard, suit scoring the concrete as he slid. "Takra, we can hold another ten," he said. "No more." He sounded like a man measuring his own death.

"You hold another ten," Jude said, "only if it buys us eleven."

Revra inclined his head one degree. Respect, or something adjacent to it.

The attack hit like weather. The outer wall buckled near the east bay door, a wedge of heavy armor pushing like a bull through a fence line. Concrete dust blew hot and fine. Men with shields flowed into the breach, rifles up and steady in a way that said training had done its job.

The first mercenary to meet them died before he knew he was in a kill box.

"Move," Nireva said, and Rakkar obliged, because surviving has a grammar. They rushed into the driving seats and started the engines.

Jude cut Ella's binds, and they were halfway to the recon ship when *Kareth* stepped into the corridor. He looked wrong in a way that made the wrongness hard to name: limping but fast, jaw tight but somehow loose around the eyes, as if sleep and sanity had both been rationed and denied in the same breath.

He did not aim at Jude. He pivoted left, took two strides, and drove Ella back against a wall. The gun found her temple like a thought.

The hallway's noise compressed into a thin, mean silence. The metal surface was cold against Ella's left hip and shoulder. She held those shoulders square because fear never helped her yet.

"Takra," Kareth said. He made Vael's title sound like a demand for proof. "Look at what you've done. Look at what you've become." His eyes were fever-bright. "You protect her. You talk to humans like equals. You are a stranger to your own kind."

Jude's hand hovered a breath away from his holster. If he moved wrong, Kareth would twitch; if Kareth twitched, Ella would die.

"I am what I need to be for us to win," Jude said. "Let her go."

Kareth smiled the way men smile when they finally find a confession they like. "You say 'win' like a human says 'fair.' Vael would never."

"I am Vael," Jude said, flat enough to shake. He let the old consonants sit inside his mouth and harden. "And I don't repeat myself."

Kareth's eyes widened a fraction. Shock or joy. It was hard to tell with men like him.

"Then prove it," he hissed. He shook Ella once, hard, like people do with objects when they don't trust they're real. "Clean your house."

There was a scrape above them, rubber on steel, boot on catwalk, and then Cassie's breath steadied. She had a line on the scene from the metal grating that ran along the corridor's top edge, a sniper's gallery that probably served engineers who never expected to be shot at. She hadn't meant to overhear. Now she couldn't unknow it.

Was it possible that those possessed could become unpossessed? And Jude was in fact the human Jude, or at least a Jude that retained some resemblance to his humanity? All the tip-offs came like a puzzle piece clicked into place, the image suddenly obvious.

Kareth's weight shifted. Ella felt it, the pressure on her skull lifting for half a heartbeat as his attention jackknifed between weapon and pride. She drove her elbow back with everything she had. His breath left him with a wet sound. The gun flinched. The shot went wide, through skin and muscle, hot, tearing across the top of her shoulder. Heat blossomed and went cold at the edges; the room got too bright.

Jude's weapon cleared leather and fired. Kareth dove behind a steel cabinet that had never been designed to stop bullets and did a poor job of pretending. Sparks wrote brief flowers across the metal.

"Move!" Cassie shouted down, and her voice cut through the smoke like something human in a room that had stopped being.

She fired, precise, controlled—three rounds, tight group, each a little lower than the last to force Kareth to drop his center of gravity and lose his angles. He got small; she had him cornered.

Jude moved without thinking that he was moving. He got his arms under Ella—she swore, because pain has its own language—and pulled her into the hall. She bled onto him in a way that made the word blood feel inadequate.

"Cassie," he shouted. "Come."

"Not with him here," she said, eyes on the cabinet, gun steady. Her mouth didn't tremble. "Go."

He didn't say thank you, because there wasn't a word in any tongue that would have been enough. He nodded once—their language—and ran.

Rakkar's charges started their countdown. He felt it through the floor, a drum still distant but on its way.

In Bay One, the recon craft's systems spun to a higher tone. Nireva strapped and glared briefly at Jude as he carried in Ella, as he set her into the med sling; it tightened around her like a bandage that knew how to think. She hissed once, then made that tight sound again, the one people make when they include someone else in their pain without meaning to. He hated that sound. He liked that he still hated things.

Out in the yard, Revra dragged a comrade to cover and barked in the old cadence. "Cut back!" He checked the fuel readouts; he didn't need a screen to read, and then lied to himself about how much more he could do.

The breach in the east wall bloomed wider. Soldiers flowed through it, shoulders back, rifles up, feet light. Their world had rules. The recon suits broke rules. The collision looked like history happening in real time.

Rakkar's monitor showed the grid lighting as the explosives woke: a schematic of the complex overlaid with blinking points—hallway joins, load-bearing corners, cable trunks, fuel lines, research hoods, server racks. Every point is a small decision. Every small decision is a very large one.

He tapped a key. Somewhere deep, a heavy door slammed open to create a pressure path. Somewhere else, a safety interlock refused to disengage and then thought better of it as the override insisted.

"Now," Jude said.

"Now," Rakkar agreed.

They didn't look at Nireva. There are moments when asking permission is the same as asking to die.

Revra took a last step back, squad on his flank. He lifted his gauntlets. In the dark of the visor, a cursor blipped across a map of light and came to rest on a symbol none of the human systems in this state would have understood.

"Detonate on my mark," Rakkar warned into his channel.

"You detonate on mine," Revra snapped, and Jude smiled despite himself because some hierarchies carry across all worlds.

Bullets wrote fireflies across the suits' plating. The humans shouted something Jude didn't need to understand. The world went very quiet in the way it does just before a lot of it becomes loud.

"Now," Revra said, and Rakkar pushed them all over a cliff.

The first explosions were inside the walls, not outside, not even at the joints where men expected demolition to happen. Heat built in the arteries and then ripped outward, flaying plaster, sending rebar whipping like snakes. A hallway vanished in dust. A lab hood became shrapnel and then air. The east wall didn't so much cave as decide it no longer felt like it had to participate in load bearing and fell apart in a stream.

Outside, the ground bucked. Tanks rocked like ships in a bad tide. Men stumbled. A helicopter pilot swore into his mic and pulled pitch as a column of heat clawed upward.

Bay One shook a long, low shake like a dog shrugging off water. The recon craft lifted off its struts with a reluctance that felt like physics negotiating with pride.

Cassie kept her focus amid the smoke and fire, as she kept Kareth pinned until one of her rounds cut the corner off the cabinet and sent a stream of cheap three-ring binders fluttering into the air like very unhelpful birds.

He took the distraction and ran. She tracked him, fired, missed by inches as he darted behind a forklift. It didn't matter. Her job wasn't to kill him. Her job was to stop him from killing anyone else for the next breath and the one after that.

A beam collapsed in the corridor behind her. She flinched, then threw herself into the smoke, half-crawling, half-running toward the sound of men trying to hold a line with willpower alone. She didn't look back. Looking back is for when you survive.

The recon ship nosed into the gap, which wasn't big enough. It clipped concrete with a noise that made every tooth in their heads ache. Then the craft shouldered through, heat washing along its skin in sheets, and found clean air. They pulled up hard. Gravity tried to make opinions. The ship ignored them.

Below, the complex turned into light, a hot, hungry pillar that wrote a message into the heavens: You are too late.

In the yard, Revra raised his gauntlet one more time and dragged the shield matrix like a curtain, buying a last six seconds to break contact. His last surviving crew member took a heavy round through a knee joint and fell, armor screeching as it scraped across concrete. Revra put a hand on the fallen suit's chest and threw—actually threw—the man in armor as heavy as an engine block as far as possible with the hope he would fall outside the blast radius. The suit landed wrong, rolled, but still showed signs of life.

Revra turned, took one step forward into the assault, and let his gauntlets glow white.

The blast wave took him and turned his shape into a piece of night.

"*We remain,*" the old liturgy repeated in Jude's head as he observed the explosion from above. "*We return.*"

The recon ship climbed.

The yard shook, rattling glass and gut alike. Cassie crouched behind the armored carrier and tasted dust and metal on her tongue. She steadied her breath.

The suits weren't just strong; they were a preview. Multiply this by millions; you didn't get a battle, you got extinction. She wouldn't live long enough to see it play out. She only hoped Jude would make it count.

Syria returned to her for a moment, the sun on broken roofs, the crack of rifles that came too fast to count. Morales, who laughed at her bad Arabic and never came home. Quinn, hauling two radios because no one else could be trusted. Lynn, bleeding out in her lap while she promised lies she wanted to believe. Their faces had blurred with time, but now the glow of alien weapons seared them sharp again, burning against American steel.

She had told herself she'd never see them again, not really. But here, in the fire and wreckage, she felt them near, shadows at her shoulder, steadying her hands, whispering the one thing she had never let herself believe: that it was all right.

Nireva swallowed whatever she had been about to say. She folded her hands together tightly and stared straight ahead. There was a line of blood along her wrist where a shard of something had kissed her and she hadn't noticed. Rakkar didn't speak either. His eyes were on the schematic in his lap, as if he could look hard enough to keep the whole building down.

Ella's breath rattled. The sling adjusted pressure the way a hand does when it learns a person. Jude checked her shoulder—ugly entry, messy, high enough to scrape bone, but not so high the lungs were asked to join the argument. He should have felt relief. It came out like anger because that's how relief often arrives in men who think they don't deserve it.

"Stay with me," he said, and she opened one eye and rolled it at him because that's how she had always spoken when blood was the subject.

Outside the cockpit, the clouds gave way to a sky the color that poets like, and then to the other color, the black that isn't black, because it holds too much. The stars were there and wrong in the way that stars are wrong when you're above the air that shifts them.

"Course?" Rakkar asked because he liked to pretend questions still had meaning.

"Up," Jude said, and nobody laughed.

Behind them, the fire dwindled to a complex of coals and collapsed. Cassie might be counting the dead somewhere under that smoke because someone had to. She might be writing the list that no one would be allowed to read if she lived.

In the white expanse, Vael paced the bars, once, twice. *"She saved you—us—from the certain death you got us into,"* he said. It sounded like contempt. Jude wasn't sure who it was for.

"She bought us a decision," Jude said. *"We used it."*

"Always the bookkeeper," Vael said, and the bars hummed.

The recon ship cut a clean line upward.

"Jude?" Ella murmured. Her voice fuzzed with pain and morphine and the kind of tired you only get from being betrayed by your own body.

"I'm here," he said. It sounded like a promise. It was only a location.

"Don't let go," she said.

He shut his eyes for one second and let an entire decade pass over him. He would break every rule he had ever written for himself to avoid lying to her directly. He tightened his hand around hers and didn't make a sound.

Below them, the flat dark of Nebraska began to curve. Above them, points of light shifted on lines no human agency had drawn, and a space between things that had always been far apart got measurable.

Jude reflected back on the Hampshire incident that had changed his life forever. He thought about Cassie in a corridor with a gun, a promise, and the sort of spine that wins wars and never gets statues. He thought about Kareth in a pocket of smoke, coughing on his own certain demise. He thought about Revra's gauntlets and the way some men meet their end like a full stop, not a comma, and had mixed feelings about an Aethero dying for his sake.

Two years of running, of narrow escapes and luck that felt like strategy until it broke, yet the pods were gone. Burned, broken, buried. For once, the math leaned his way: Aethrie might have to turn its eyes backward instead of forward.

He'd need to deal with Nireva and Rakkar at some point, too.

For now, he was with Ella, and in that moment, it felt more important than saving the world.

"Hold on," he said to her.

"Always," she said, and gave him a look that wasn't brave or tragic, just exactly what she had left that wasn't pain.

Suddenly, the craft's alarm system started blazing.

"What's happening?"

Rakkar's face changed first. Not fear, not quite. More like recognition. "Autopilot isn't an error. It's a recall. In an emergency, Aethrie drags its nearby vessels home. And it's dragging us now."

"No," Jude heard Vael in a worried whisper. *"this can only mean one thing."*

Nireva turned to Jude with a dreaded look, the first time he had seen her lose her cunning gaze. "Aethrie is under attack."

PART V:

THE ACCORDS

Chapter 22: BEYOND EARTH

The checkpoint was a coffin with windows.

Admiral Serres leaned back in his cradle seat and stared at nothing. That was most of what checkpoint duty gave him: nothing, repeated until it looked like eternity. A line of patrol ships rode lazy arcs on the outskirts of the solar system, their beacons dimmed, their formations correct to the decimal. Nothing ever broke them. Nothing ever crossed.

Serres pressed his tongue against his teeth. This was not what he had signed up for. He had been trained in fleet school for doctrine, engagements, and battles that left wakes across entire quadrants. Instead, he was parked in Sol, one of the backwaters of the Assembly maps, a natural reserve for a primitive race with nothing worth fighting for except boredom.

His homeworld and his race, which made up the majority of his fleet, were not considered fully integrated members of the Assembly, but rather allied only from a military perspective. Low trust, low prestige. Expendable in Assembly eyes. And so they only ever received the low-quality assignments.

Serres dreamed of combat. Of the chance to prove himself in fire. He had read too many old stories of admirals whose names carved cycles into history, while his own logbooks filled with cycles recorded only in silence.

Then the flare came.

"Contact." The word was sharp enough to make the deck crew sit straighter. "Vector inbound, masked signature, breaking from eclipse at Kora-5. Not Assembly. Not civilian. Shape matches,"

"Say it," Serres snapped.

The officer's voice cracked. "Aethero recon craft."

The boredom vanished. Serres' veins lit like wire. He almost laughed. "Finally."

He sat forward, crisp now, the jadedness burned off him like slag in a furnace. "Signal the net. Collapse the perimeter. We will not let this one through."

His orders spilled clean as the screens flashed up, giving him clarity of the weaknesses of the Aethrie's positioning within the gas giant's orbit. "Two wedges forward. Pincer from high orbit. Push it into the well. I want Jupiter's pull on our side. Gravity makes a better accomplice than any gun." He learnt that from one of his favorite stories.

No hesitation from the crew now. Thrusters lit across the fleet, small flares against the giant planet's storms. Doctrine clicked into place. Serres watched the formations shift, the geometry of war assembling itself out of boredom's ashes. This was doctrine, yes, but finally doctrine with teeth.

He let himself smile, thin and sharp. This was his moment. This was what checkpoint duty had been waiting to deliver him: not silence, not boredom, but honor.

The recon ship crossed the blue, then the edge of blue, into the vast. The Earth below did what it always does when someone leaves it: it pretended not to care.

Inside the cabin, the three uninjured hosts—the woman who wanted to own a country, the man who wanted to solve it, and the man who wanted to save it or maybe break it—shared the kind of silence that changes a room into a confession.

Jude lay back in a resigned posture. It was ideal that the enemy he had faced for so long could finally be defeated. It was not ideal, however, that he and Ella were being pulled up towards the worst of it.

The recon ship bucked under them like a horse that had already chosen its rider. Jude gripped the edge of the console until the lines burned into his palms.

Rakkar angled the display. The trajectory carved itself bright against the dark. Toward the mass. Toward the storm. Toward Jupiter.

"It's not just the enemy fleet that's the problem," Nireva said. Her voice carried a tension that sounded very little like control. "Look."

She spread the feed wide. Aethrie loomed on the edge of the gas giant's horizon, vast as a world, its outer ribs straining under the tug of the gravitational well. Engines burned in fits and throbs, shoving against a pull that could have swallowed continents. Around it, light speared and shattered: Assembly fire, disciplined and endless.

The planetoid was caught. Fighting a planet's pull on one side and a fleet's push on the other.

Jude's eyes rested on Aethrie and took it all in. His stomach clenched so tight it hurt. This was his sworn enemy for the past twenty-five months. His plan to remove the threat was in play. He should feel victorious, and he did, but Vael's silence in the expanse was not triumph, and somehow Jude found himself borrowing that silence. These were his enemies, yet they were also people chasing the memory of home.

Assembly fighters streaked like silver needles on the displays, their trails etched clean against Jupiter's storm bands. Missiles unreeled in disciplined lines. Countermeasures flared from Aethrie's hull, glimmering barriers of light that bent trajectories just wide enough. But not all. Impacts ripped craters into armor older than empires.

Ella groaned low, her arm throbbed in rhythm with the alarms, sling biting deeper as if it too resented survival. "What's happening?" she whispered.

"War," Jude said, and the word tasted like stone.

Quick-thinking Nireva gave each of them a booster shot, which allowed them temporary immunity from the Aethrie microbiome environment, which would now be foreign to their homo sapiens bodies; later, they would still need the fuller vaccine impact to give them a more permanent resistance.

The fluid stung under Jude's skin, metallic and sharp, as if the body already knew it was being asked to accept something unnatural. Ella flinched but steadied herself, her jaw locked. The dose seemed to buy her strength she didn't own anymore.

The ship approached a docking section opposite to where the majority of the Assembly-allied fleet was. As they landed and the door opened, Jude—or rather Vael—saw a familiar face in Lyren, approaching them and followed by a small group of soldiers and medics.

"Takra, you made it back," she sounded relieved. Her voice was pitched for ceremony, but Jude caught the fracture of genuine fear beneath it. Even here, soldiers wore relief like weakness.

He signaled to the health workers to take Ella and noted to them that she was on a booster. Assured of Ella's safety, he turned back to Lyren.

"Lyren, brief us." And briefed them she did.

It was not great. For stealth purposes, Aethrie had been stationed as close as it could to Jupiter without getting into its gravitational pull. For cycles, it had avoided any Assembly contact, and this grew into overconfidence. The maps she pushed onto the hologram showed the planetoid's ribs trembling, its massive engines firing in uneven surges, half of their output spent simply countering Jupiter's hunger. Each burst lit the planet's clouds below in lightning shadows.

They believe a random signal had been sent by one of the recon ships from Earth, which alerted this Assembly fleet.

A single Assembly fleet would not have usually been an issue for Aethrie. Still, the fleet's ambush and tactics were unexpected, and they had successfully pinned down the planetoid in a precarious position where it was having to use most of its energy to fight against a crash landing into the red storm.

The situation was so dire that they had the High Circle evacuated to Ganymede, escorted by five fleets, one from each clan.

"Cowards!" cursed Vael from the expanse. His contempt echoed so loudly Jude felt his own ribs rattle with it.

The generals leading the fleets of Vael's and Nireva's respective clans dialled in.

"Takra, Nireva, we are pleased to see you back, in your new bodies, unfortunately not in better circumstances," bellowed one of them, and the others chimed in agreement.

They spoke of what had been done so far: burning through reserve fuel to keep Aethrie from tipping, throwing half their arsenal into flak screens that did little but buy minutes, not hours. One clan had already lost a third of its escort ships. Another grudgingly admitted that morale was buckling; their soldiers had been trained to fight other fleets, not a planet itself.

Jude deliberated on what he could do and what he *would* do.

The expanse

Jude reflected on the sight of Aethrie struggling to break from its cage, which it found itself in, not unlike the prisoner he had in his mind. The vast bulk of the worldship flexed against Jupiter's invisible chains. It looked like a drowning giant, engines flailing as waves of gravity dragged it closer to the storm wall. Every shudder of its hull was mirrored in the white expanse; Vael pacing, pressing, raging against the bars. The two cages reflected each other.

"This is it," he told Vael. *"Your world breaks itself on Jupiter. My people will live. I've won."*

Vael roared back from the white cage. *"Fool. If Aethrie dies, the Assembly claims your Earth next. You think they stop at our corpses? You are now an unneeded emerging threat with your knowledge of what exists outside your system. They will cut your species clean out of the sky and leave you nothing."*

"Better than bending to you?" Jude hissed aloud. *"I'm willing to take my chances with a low probability of an Assembly invasion, versus a certain one from your kind.*

"Help me," Vael demanded, but pleading. His voice cracked with something Jude had never heard in it before—fear, raw and unvarnished. *"Save them, our forty million people, and I swear this: I will turn our generals. Earth will be spared. Without me, you face them and the Assembly both. With me, you choose which enemy you keep."*

The words burned like molten metal. Forty million, an entire civilization, held in his palm for judgment. Jude wanted to spit, to say their lives were not his to save or end. But they were. Because the moment he refused, Jupiter and the Assembly would finish the work for him.

He saw Ella, pale but breathing on the med-bench. He saw Cassie, holding a line she would never leave. He saw Earth, fragile and unknowing, still turning on its axis like none of this existed.

"You ask me to save your people so mine can live?" Jude said, his voice low. *"Then you promise me more than survival. You swear on your name, on your cage, on whatever gods Aethrie still pretends to; Earth will be left alone."*

Vael leaned to the bars, eyes bright with something beyond anger. *"I swear it. On my clan. On my blood. Let me out, and I will cut the Assembly's hand before it ever reaches Earth.*

For the first time since Hampshire, Jude felt choice collapse into inevitability. The war he thought he was ending had just begun, but with a new weapon, one that carried both risk and promise.

And then Vael added, softly but with the weight of a vow: *"Let this be our accords."*

The word lodged in Jude's chest like molten iron, both wound and promise.

Outside in the real world, missiles streak and countermeasures bloom like false stars. The void between Aethrie and Jupiter lit like a sky on fire, every flash another second stolen from catastrophe. And in the white cage, Jude's silence became a decision.

In the medical bay, Ella lay on a narrow cot, her sling pressing a steady weight into her shoulder. She should have been unconscious, but the ship carried its own rhythm, and it kept her awake. Through the reinforced glass of the bulkhead, she could see the wounded brought in; Aethero soldiers stripped of helmets and armor, faces pale from strain, voices hoarse from giving orders.

They looked human. Not metaphor, not resemblance, but human. Faces she could have seen in London, or Washington, or Shanghai: eyes too tired, mouths pressed into the same shapes fear and duty always pressed them into.

A medic guided two children past her line of sight. They couldn't have been more than five or six. A boy clung to his sister's sleeve with white-knuckled fingers, trying not to cry, his small chest heaving as he fought to breathe like a soldier. The girl's lips were pressed thin, as if she believed that if she didn't break, maybe the world wouldn't either. Their eyes darted to the sound of every distant impact, wide and terrified, and Ella's stomach folded in on itself.

One of the medics caught her staring. He had freckles under his eyes, the same as her brother had. For a second, her throat closed, because it wasn't just soldiers who bled in these wars; it was families.

It was children who should never have been anywhere near a battlefield.

They weren't monsters or aliens in any way her brain wanted them to be. They were *us*.

And if millions more were waiting to come through the gates Jude had been trying to close, she finally understood the weight of Cassie's warnings, of Jude's choices, and why none of this could ever be simple.

Ella shut her eyes, but the knowledge followed her into the dark: the battle for Earth was not against strangers. It was against mirrors.

Chapter 23:
JUPITER IGNITES

The void erupted.

Serres leaned forward in his cradle seat as the first volleys lit against Aethrie's hull. Missiles etched clean lines across the storm bands of Jupiter, fire stitching itself into doctrine. He felt alive in a way boredom had never permitted. This was the moment he would carve his name into history; not by holding a line, but by forcing an enemy world into the pull of a god.

Yet even as the fleet closed in, something stirred. Aethrie shifted, not as prey, but as something that remembered it had teeth.

Rakkar was the first to see it. Buried in the worldship's command nexus, his fingers danced across the console, bending frequencies until countermeasures bloomed ahead of Assembly salvos. He didn't fire a shot; he moved shadows, tricking guidance arrays into believing their prey had already been destroyed. Rockets tore themselves apart chasing ghosts. He allowed himself a thin smile.

"*Vekan thuaral!*" Out came the Aethero rallying cry. *We ascend by fire!*

Nireva seized the opening. Her clan's fleets swept in from the lower arc, small craft diving through the slipstream like knives through silk. Where Serres expected brute resistance, he found precision ambush. Her voice cut through the tactical net: "Strike what they don't guard. Leave them chasing echoes." Her ships obeyed. An entire wedge of inexperienced Assembly frigates staggered as their engines took hits from angles their doctrine hadn't predicted.

Serres slammed his fist against the arm of his chair. "Hold formation!" he barked, fury bleeding into every syllable. His officers moved with discipline, but he could taste the doubt now. The Aethero weren't breaking; they were turning.

Vael pressed to the bars in the white expanse, his voice a low thunder in Jude's skull. "*Now you see. They taught us to bend stars, not to kneel before them. Let me guide your hand, and I'll gut their admiral before he even knows he's lost.*"

For once, Jude didn't resist. He opened his mind to Vael's push, and the flood was immediate, battle rhythms older than empires, maneuvers drilled into the marrow of Aethero officers. He saw vectors bend in ways human doctrine had never imagined. He saw how to turn Jupiter's pull into an advantage.

"Shift the outer shields," Jude ordered aloud, his voice carrying the steel of command. Rakkar relayed it without question, and the larger recon ships outside adjusted, their lattice glowing like a second skin. Missiles screamed past harmlessly, tricked into spirals by the shift in field geometry.

Then Vael moved deeper. Through Jude's hands, he drew the fleets into a maneuver no human doctrine could have conceived. Instead of resisting Jupiter's pull, the Aethero craft let themselves fall, deliberately, skimming the edge of the gravity well like stones across black water. The Assembly ships followed, hungry for the kill, only to have their own trajectories turned against them.

Every lesson Jude had ever learned told him to fight gravity, not surrender to it. His instincts recoiled; this was suicide. And yet, as Vael's intent pressed through the bars, he saw the shape beneath the madness. The drop was a lever. The planet's pull wasn't death; it was a weapon, if you knew where to cut it loose. Jude's human muscles and Vael's alien memory aligned for one suspended heartbeat, and his hands moved as if they had always known the rhythm.

Vael had plotted the descent not as retreat but as a trap: a sling-turn, converting the plunge into raw velocity, then flaring side thrusters to whip Aethrie's ships back out of the well at impossible angles.

Fire meant for them tore into their pursuers instead, lances of light crossing into friendly hulls before Serres could shout the correction. It was audacity disguised as collapse, which worked because only a Takra's mind would dare it.

Serres swore as his attack lines collapsed. "Impossible," he muttered, but already his board was bleeding red where Aethero's strikes slipped through.

Nireva watched Serres' ships stutter from her fleet's bridge and fall back. For the first time, she believed Vael's promise of turning this battle. She let herself whisper, almost reverent: "Takra Vael returns in fire."

Rakkar's voice cut into the comms, taut with triumph. "Their doctrine is brittle. Press here." He flared a hologram across the net, highlighting a seam in Serres' formation. Jude—Vael—gave the order, and the Aethero fleets pivoted with lethal grace.

The clash was no longer prey against predator. It was knife against throat.

Jude braced as his fleet shuddered under near impact. He felt Vael's fury transmute into strategy; sharp, clean, relentless. Together, unwilling allies, they steered the Aethero's counterstroke.

On the Assembly flagship, Serres realized too late that his 'lucky kill' had turned. The recon ship he thought was prey had guided an ancient empire back into its own strength. For the first time in his career, he tasted the truth he had craved: not glory, but defeat.

But Serres was not a man who would accept silence as his epitaph. If he could not drag Aethrie into Jupiter's grave, he would carve his name in another way. His sensors pinged, five Aethero fleets stationed in orbit of Ganymede, guarding what every officer whispered about but never said aloud: the High Circle. The mythical core of Aethrie's rule. If the Council were truly there, then destroying them would alter the course of history.

He stood from his cradle seat, unstrapped, his voice cutting across the comms with a sharpness that made every officer look up.

"My brothers and sisters, sons and daughters. Today we are not forgotten."

His voice carried through the fleet, patched onto every channel.

"They stationed us at the edges because they thought we were lesser, because our race was allied only in body, not in honor. They meant us to wither in silence, to fade without leaving a mark. But the galaxy remembers those who burn."

His tone grew hotter, steadier.

"Before us lies not just an enemy, but their heart. The Aethero High Circle hides behind Ganymede's stone. Break them, and we carve our names into the marrow of history. Break them, and they will know our people are not slaves to Assembly scraps. If we fall, we fall remembered. If we die, we die as the spear that struck the gods themselves."

The crew straightened. On dozens of bridges across his fleet, men and women raised their fists, voices answering with a ragged cheer. For one moment, Serres' fleet believed. Believed that death was not the end, but the monument.

He sat again, a thin smile carved deep. "New heading," he ordered. "Full burn to Ganymede. All ships. Now."

Engines roared to life, battered hulls turning from Jupiter's maelstrom. Across the net, the five Aethero clans guarding the moon reacted with scorn. "One fleet against five? Madness. Hold your ground, Assembly."

But Serres was already laughing, the sound like iron tearing. "One fleet is enough. One fleet with nothing left to lose."

The Assembly formation tightened, ships locking into ramming vectors. For one heartbeat, the void was silent, waiting. Then Serres gave the order.

"Engage."

The Assembly fleet surged forward like a single blade, ignoring fire, ignoring attrition, engines screaming white-hot as they closed on the Ganymede perimeter. The Aethero defenders scrambled, volleys cutting into hulls, but Serres' line did not break. They drove straight through the storm, aiming not to survive, but to collide.

The first impact bloomed like a sunburst, an Assembly cruiser tearing itself apart against an Aethero dreadnought. Explosions cascaded across the formation, one detonation feeding the next, until the space above Ganymede was a crown of fire. In the chaos, signals spiked and vanished, the kind of loss reports that meant whole delegations were gone.

On his bridge, seconds before the shockwave consumed him, Serres closed his eyes. Not defeat, he thought. Not silence. "*They will speak of this. My race will not be forgotten.*"

And then his flagship struck, and Serres' ambition became a pyre visible across half the solar system.

The impact came in waves of light and silence. Serres' fleet folded itself into the Aethero escort like a blade driven to the hilt, hulls shattering against hulls, reactors bursting into suns that burned for seconds and yet scarred forever. Ganymede's horizon lit as though the moon itself had caught fire. The crust shuddered, thin geysers venting skyward where the impacts tore deep.

On the command boards across Aethrie's fleets, signals winked out one after another. Not Assembly. Not Serres. The beacons were theirs—their escorts, their guardians, and among them, the signatures that had marked the Circle's convoy.

Gone.

The silence that followed was the kind that rewrote worlds. For the first time in cycles uncounted, Aethrie—and the Aethero—had no High Circle.

Chapter 24: SILENT THRONES

The chamber had been built for ceremony and repurposed for war.

It sat deep in Aethrie's government complex, a ring of black stone interrupted by a single small table of living alloy in the center. Vents breathed a clean, cold draft that smelled faintly of ozone and scorched metal, the scent of engines run too hard for too long.

A hologram of Jupiter and Ganymede burned above the table, not an image so much as a wound. Arcs of wreckage glinted like broken teeth, a crown of fire still drifting outward. The space that should have been alive with signals from escorts and delegates was only silence now.

Jude stood at the near edge, palms flat. The table learned his pulse and steadied it, the way the ship steadied a pilot who didn't yet know its language. He watched leaders gather in twos and threes: clan chiefs with old scars and new calculations, admirals in battle blacks, aides who kept their eyes down and their ears open. Lyren hovered near the door, managing the flow with a soldier's courtesy; Rakkar stood ghost-still at a console, the light of a hundred feeds writing itself across his face. Nireva arrived last among the living powers—unbloodied, unbowed, the kind of composed that reads as danger.

They did not sit. There was nothing to sit on. The Aethero liked to make decisions while alert and standing, and it also had the benefit of keeping meetings efficient.

Whispers arrived first, crossing the floor like drafts in an old house.

The Assembly fleet was wounded; why not finish them?

Should have intercepted before Ganymede.

Vael returns, and the Council dies.

Jude let them pass through him. He felt Vael listening too, the way a storm listens for the hill it will choose to break itself on.

Lyren struck the chime. The sound was thin and absolute. It pulled eyes to the center.

"Takra," she said, and the title landed in the room with a weight you didn't earn so much as inherit. "The clans are present."

Jude—Vael—stepped into the open. He did not raise his hands. He didn't need to. The posture did the work: chin level, shoulders set, gaze steady enough that it made the floor feel flatter. The murmurs memoed themselves into silence.

"We have names for our clans," he said. "Keep them. But you *had* masters. They burned."

A shift moved through the room, half shock, half recognition that no one else would say it aloud.

"Ganymede is not an accident," he went on. "It is a proof. We were taught for cycles to accept caution as a strategy. We were told to balance the ledger of risk with a trembling hand. An enemy with nothing left to lose taught us the shape of that mistake in fire." He let the hologram rotate, bright wreckage spinning, then stilled it with a glance. "Now you will learn a new language."

He let the silence stretch, then cut it clean:

"The Council's plan to reclaim Old Aethrie was also not a strategy; it was vanity. Based on knowledge of many star-cycles old. The planet's population is more technologically advanced than we thought. More connected. We are still much better, but we are only forty million strong; they are eight billion, with atomic bombs enough to make Old Aethrie unrecognisable many times over. To strike Old Aethrie while the Assembly still draws breath is to fight two wars with one blade. That is not a strength. I will not let our people commit suicide."

His voice lowered, the timbre pulling every ear in the chamber forward.

"You will keep your names, your regiments, your fleets. But you will not keep the habits of the dead. The Assembly attacked us; the longstanding truce or cold war is over. We know they have increasingly and aggressively expanded their alliance network with the intention of choking our movements and the livelihood of our people. We are today in a different universe than the one our High Circle knew. The Assembly is an imminent threat.

He then attempted to inspire hope.

But the Assembly also bled today. They can bleed again. That is where we strike, until the threat behind us is ash, not shadow. Then, and only then, will the horizon be ours to choose."

He could feel Rakkar behind him, watching every verb.

An admiral from the far arc, a broad-shouldered man with a scar that ran like a river from temple to jaw, stepped forward without permission. "This new language you mention, whose name does it end with?" His voice didn't seek permission either. "We answer to the High Circle. They are..." He caught himself. The word gone doesn't make a sound when you swallow it. "They were our law."

Jude met the man's eyes. "Your law fled to a moon in cowardice. The Assembly called that dare. The Assembly writes its own laws in teeth. You can follow ghosts, or you can follow the fire that still answers when you call it. Choose."

The admiral's jaw worked once. He stepped back. Not submission. Positioning.

From the second circle, another voice, lighter, carrying an edge you only get from running ships instead of rooms. "There are questions that require answers, Takra," said a woman with cropped hair and a bearing like a blade. "At Ganymede, after Aethrie was freed, the home fleets chased Jupiter-side threats and left the moon to escorts. If orders were misread, we correct doctrine. If orders were not misread..." She didn't finish it. She didn't need to.

Her eyes were not the only ones that lifted toward Jude.

In the white expanse, Vael pressed his palms to the bars. *"Say nothing,"* he said without sound.

Jude let the silence kneel for him before he broke it. "The admiral of the Assembly fleet now gone was desperate enough to bleed victory out of death," he said. "He turned his fleet into a weapon our doctrine didn't name. The moment that weapon declared itself, we had a different choice: spend the strength of Aethrie chasing a knife already falling, or break the hand that threw it. We chose the hand." He kept his face still. He did not add, *and we chose what the knife would cut.*

A rumor of understanding moved. It wasn't an agreement. It was the acceptance of a shape in the fog.

Nireva, silent so far to properly read the room and assess her options, stepped into the open, her eyes catching light like polished stone. "We will memorialize the Council," she said, voice crisp as a plan. "We will keep their names alive in the schools. And then we will not be them." She turned slightly, enough to address the room without turning away from Jude. "The Assembly now knows we have teeth. And we know they will not tolerate a predator in their reserve. If we turn toward Earth now, they close the jaws on our backs. Two fronts, as Vael eloquently put. That is folly disguised as courage."

A beat, and then the question in the air answered itself. Heads turned toward Jude again, some grudging, some hungry.

He let them wait one second longer, then gave them a plan and a vow.

"We do not reclaim Earth," he said. The words hit like cold water. "Not now. Not while our enemies move on the other side and expand their influence sphere. Not while our engines still reek of strain. We do not make war on two horizons and call it strength.

We consolidate. We draw our breath. We turn the blade and give the Assembly what they thought they gave us today."

He let the hologram shift at a brush of his hand. Patrol routes spiraled across a map of Assembly choke points. For the past several cycles, they had been obstacles in isolation, as Aethrie moved in stealth, avoiding them. Now, on the map, they aligned into vertebrae of a single spine.

"We break their spine where it bends," he said. "Their checkpoints. Their message relays. The small wars that keep their big fleets from coalescing around us. We write to them in the language their destroyed fleet chose, a language with no word for mercy and a perfect memory for debt. And when they look away from us and this system to save their throats, we will decide the rest."

A low exhale went through the chamber. Calculations began to rewrite themselves behind the eyes.

"Promises," the scarred admiral said, because the room needed at least one more objection. "You promise Old Aethrie its reprieve now. Later, you will promise us glory. Later, you will change the order of those promises. That is the way of leaders."

Jude didn't blink. "I will write this promise in the only way you still believe in," he said. "In the names of ships. In the fuel, we do not burn. In the gates, we do not open. If I break it, you will remove me, and that will be the end of that story."

In the expanse, Vael's laugh was short and unkind. "*You threaten your own throat to buy time. Brave. Wasteful. Effective.*"

The far side of the ring stuttered. Then a single figure stepped forward past his own circle, an older man with eyes that had seen too many salvage lists and not enough funerals for the people who should have been in them. He stopped two paces from Jude and did a thing that hadn't been done in that room since before it had been repurposed for war.

He knelt. No flourish. No speech. He set his palms to the floor and bowed his head until the nape of his neck showed to every hand that might choose to cut it.

"The Fifth Regiment," he said, voice steady with authority as his clan's Takra. "We bend to Takra Vael. Not because we love him. Because we love Aethrie, and it still breathes with his leadership."

The decision moved through the fifth circle like water, finding the lowest point. Two admirals in his shadow stepped forward and mirrored the kneel. Then two more. Within a breath, an entire corner of the room had lowered itself to the stone.

Nireva watched something open in the air, something with velocity. She did not hesitate. She stepped out so cleanly it read like choreography. The line of her spine was a statement; the tilt of her head was a message placed in forty ears at once. She went down, not all the way, sharp enough to suggest choice, deep enough to make it undeniable. "The Third Regiment stands with Takra Vael," she said. "And with Aethrie, so long as his word stands." She let that clause gleam.

She didn't need to look behind her. The admirals of her clan were already moving. Men and women who had raised their ships through the last hours of fire bent their knees because they could read a map, and this was what all maps do when the hill is steep enough. Their actual Takra, a man who had survived by saying "perhaps" as if it were a strategy, stood trapped in the eddy of his own authority. He held a breath too long. Then he went down, face pale, and bowed so low it looked like he was testing whether the floor would forgive him.

Vael's own regiment behind him also knelt.

Three clans bent, and the room changed shape.

The remaining two chiefs stared into the future and saw the math. One lifted his chin as if height could make a tide forget its job. "If we do this," he said, "we do it to live. Not because we like the taste of your orders."

"Then live," Jude said. "And you can teach me to make them sweeter."

A bitter half-smile touched the man's mouth. He dropped to his knee. The last chief folded with him, not regal, not grand, but determined not to be the final name written into a loss.

"Vekan thuaral," they chanted thrice in unity. *We ascend by fire.*

It happened without drums. It happened without trumpets. It happened the way real shifts always do: in a changed angle of backs, in a tilt of heads. The hologram of Jupiter and Ganymede turned over them like a sky slowly forgetting to burn.

Jude—the human who dared resist Aethero possession, who dared resist Aethero invasion—was now their *sovereign,* with a throne he never yearned for.

Chapter 25:
NEW DOCTRINE

Lyren's face changed in a way Jude had only seen once, when she had thought a friend was dead and then discovered he wasn't. She hid it fast.

Rakkar didn't hide anything; he was too busy capturing three dozen streams of oath and posture and translating them into the record the future would pretend had been designed.

The murmurs had quieted. What remained was the sound of assent: ships swearing loyalty, clans bending their doctrine into new shapes, the weight of history tilting toward a single center.

Nireva found him there, in that one beat of silence, and stepped close enough to speak without being recorded. "You're either the most dangerous man I've ever backed," she said softly, "or the last good one."

"Why choose," he said, and the softness almost made it kind.

She smiled with no joy in it. "Because the world prefers being told."

Lyren's chime spared them an answer. "The clans have bent," she said for the record. "We require the shape of their bent."

Jude straightened. He let Vael's cadence step into his mouth and speak the architecture of the new order.

"The Jupiter Accords," he said. The words came easy. "They bind two things: our hand and our horizon. First, we end the war inside our own ribs. No regiment law outruns Aethrie's survival. The fleets will be braided, command rotated through competence, not lineage. Logistics first. Then guns. Then speeches."

He turned his hand, and the hologram replaced wreckage with routes. "Second, we turn outward. We break the Assembly's reach where it is thinnest and shame them where they claim they are strongest. We do not give them the fight they trained for. We give them the one they fear: a hundred cuts that never clot. Chokes. We take their reserve fleets apart before they can fold into a fist or bring them to our side as new allies. They will discover their fingers are missing if they move towards us as adversaries."

The room leaned forward as if gravity had tipped.

"Old Aethrie," he said last, because he knew they were waiting for that. "We leave it for now. We do not write our names on two skies and pretend ink is infinite. The planet we came from will keep turning and thinking the stars are only decorations. When we come back to it, we will come as rulers of our own war rather than refugees from the Assembly's. Until then, any hand that reaches for Old Aethrie without sanction forfeits its fleets."

There was a sound in the room you could mistake for respect if you wanted to. It was quieter than that. It was the sound a body makes when it decides not to die that day.

One by one, the clan chiefs spoke their assent into the net. Not all were graceful. Some turned command into a dog given a new leash. Some made a show of generosity as if they were gifting him what he had already taken. Nireva's assent was clean and professional and orchestrated so that three admirals spoke along with her, in harmony, which is a kind of threat.

When it was done, Lyren sealed it. The Jupiter Accords burned above the table for a breath and then sank into the record like a coin into deep water. The chamber leaned back, not in dissent but in something that almost resembled belief. The clans had spoken; the order was made.

They began to break apart the way men do after funerals and weddings: carefully, as if the floor might betray its patience. Nireva left first, already murmuring logistics into a line that didn't exist an hour ago. The scarred admiral took his objections with him and turned them into assignments. Rakkar remained, fingers a blur, shaping doctrine into packets.

Jude stayed. The room needed to remember his silhouette where it had done this.

In the expanse, Vael eased his grip on the bars and watched the new order place itself like a crown on a table. "*We will be blamed for Ganymede,*" he said. "*And also thanked. That is the correct balance.*"

"*We could have sent the home fleet to intercept,*" Jude thought. He kept his voice even. It didn't help.

"*They were positioned wrong for a move like that,*" Vael said. "*And positioned right for the future.*"

"*Say it,*" Jude challenged. "*Say you let it happen.*"

Vael looked at him through the white. "*When you cut out a rot, it leaves a hole,*" he said. "*If you are careful, it leaves a door. You opened this door for me. I used it for us.*"

Jude opened his eyes. The chamber had emptied down to echoes. Lyren waited by the threshold, pretending not to. "Takra," she said. "Orders?"

"Two," he replied. "Tell the shipwrights we braid the fleets by morning. No excuses. And find me a line to the med bay."

Lyren moved like a salute.

He stood under the dying light of the hologram for one more breath, then cut it with a hand. Darkness returned, proper to the room and to the hour.

He walked out into the corridor that curved toward engines, medicine, and sleep no one would get. Somewhere on the far side of that curve waited Ella, a woman with a sling who could still make him tell the truth; Rakkar, the engineer who had turned Assembly formations into confetti; and Nireva, the politician who had made a kingdom kneel without raising her voice. On the near side lay a throne built out of wreckage and vows, and the whisper that would not leave him alone:

You could have saved them.

He let it walk with him. It would have anyway.

Behind him, the new war assembled itself: routes of interdiction, lists of ships renamed for the dead, orders braided into doctrine. Somewhere out beyond the hull, Jupiter turned and pretended not to care. The Assembly would care when the first checkpoint went dark and did not answer. Earth would not care, not yet. That was part of the plan.

Jude pressed his palm to the wall as he passed, habit now, not ritual. The ship answered with a hum low as a promise.

In the white expanse, Vael watched him without comment, hands loose at his sides, eyes bright with a hunger that finally had a horizon again.

"*So this is the shape of survival,*" Jude said quietly, as if testing whether the word fit both of them.

The ship hummed back, low as a promise. Out beyond its hull, Jupiter turned, and Earth turned too, pretending not to care.

Then he rounded the curve toward the med bay and the next lie he would refuse to tell.

EPILOGUE: EMBERS

The checkpoint had been quiet for seventy-three cycles.

A single station sat adrift at the edge of Assembly territory, its beacons blinking with the patience of things designed to be ignored. Officers rotated in and out with the rhythm of boredom. Reports filed. Routes checked. Nothing ever crossed here, because nothing ever dared.

Until tonight.

"Sensor flare," called the junior officer, his voice breaking the monotony like glass dropped in water. "Not Assembly. Not civilian. Masked vector, no transponder."

The captain turned, a frown pulling lines across his face. "Origin?"

"Unknown. It bled through the filter like..." The officer's words faltered. The display spat static, then resolved into a streak of light that did not belong to any ship in their doctrine. It was a cut through the dark, precise and merciless.

Another voice on the deck: "We should raise command."

"Do it," the captain said, but his stomach had already fallen. Because the signal wasn't random, it wasn't desperate. It was deliberate, the way a knife is deliberate when it slides between ribs.

One by one, their boards lit with empties. Neighbor stations that should have answered were silent. Patrols along the sector line, gone. Not destroyed; erased.

The captain leaned close to the glass, watching the vector burn across the stars. For a heartbeat, he thought he saw the shape of a worldship—vast ribs, scars of battle still etched across its hull—but then the image fractured and scattered into decoys. The truth remained hidden.

He whispered, almost to himself: "They've come off the leash."

The officer's hands shook as he magnified the flare. Symbols bloomed in the feed, old glyphs the captain had never seen except in archived war records. A sigil, carved in light, burning against the void.

Aethero.

The station's power flickered as the flare crossed their grid. Consoles spat static. In the silence that followed, the comms unit crackled once, like a voice starting to speak, then choosing not to.

The captain tried to steady his crew, to speak orders, but his throat closed before sound could pass.

Because beyond the glass, the stars themselves seemed to move. A lattice of ships, countless and precise, filled the dark like a crown of fire.

The checkpoint didn't broadcast another report.

It didn't need to.

The Assembly would notice when one more light in its border spine went out and did not return.

A MESSAGE FROM THE AUTHOR GRATEFUL FOR YOUR FEEDBACK

★★★★★

Thank you for reading *The Black Accords: Emergence*.

Your feedback means the world and helps other readers discover the story while giving vital support to independent authors like me.

If you enjoyed the book, found it thought-provoking, or simply had fun reading it, please consider leaving a short review on Amazon. Just a few words can make a huge difference and help keep me motivated to continue writing *The Black Accords* series.

Here's how to leave a review:

1. Scan the QR code on this page to go directly to the Amazon review page.
2. Or open your Amazon Orders, find *The Black Accords: Emergence,* and click "Write a Product Review.

Scan Me

Printed in Dunstable, United Kingdom

70468248R00139